true
talents

DAVID LUBAR

A Tom Doherty Associates Book
New York

This is a work of fiction. All the characters and events portrayed
in this novel are either fictitious or are used fictitiously.

TRUE TALENTS

This book is printed on acid-free paper.

A Starscape Book
Published by Tom Doherty Associates, LLC
175 Fifth Avenue
New York, NY 10010

www.tor.com

ISBN-13: 978-0-765-30977-8
ISBN-10: 0-765-30977-7

First Edition: March 2007

Printed in the United States of America

0 9 8 7 6 5 4 3 2 1

STARSCAPE BOOKS BY DAVID LUBAR

Flip

Hidden Talents

*In the Land of the Lawn Weenies
and Other Warped and Creepy Tales*

*Invasion of the Road Weenies
and Other Warped and Creepy Tales*

For Bruce Coville,
with affection, admiration,
and a pinch of awe

PART ONE

which takes place
on the longest wednesday
any guy has ever lived through

*trying hard to focus

THE GORILLA WHO clung to the ceiling was wearing a Princeton t-shirt. It must have been an XXXXL. Exxxxelll. Exxxxelllent. That was funny. I laughed. He didn't seem to mind. He just kept playing with his cigarette lighter, sparking tiny fireworks through the air. His glasses had thick, black frames. They made him look smart. Laughing made my head spin, so I closed my eyes.

He was gone when I woke up. The walls were still rippling. They always rippled. Sometimes, they hummed movie music. They'd been painted by Vincent Van Gogh. A fuzzy man wearing a vanilla coat came in through the door and gave me a sandwich. Grilled cheese. Gorrrilllad cheese. The dark and light-brown patterns looked like George Washington. The father of our country winked at me. George Winkington. Everyone knows he washed down the cherry cheese.

The cheese was sort of tangy.

Tangy?

That's a taste. I rubbed my tongue across my front teeth and tried to remember the last time I'd tasted something. I knew I'd had other meals. I could remember the clack of a plastic knife and fork against a tray. But I couldn't remember any tastes or smells. It was all cardboard. I stared at my right hand. My fingers grew longer. I stared harder. They snapped back. But the crumbs on my fingertips kept singing. It was a nice song about fractions.

I finished my sandwich and took another nap.

The walls didn't ripple at all when I woke. Picasso had snuck in and painted over Van Gogh's work. Vincent would be furious about that. Picasso better keep an eye on his ears.

I sat up to look around. My body got there first, so I waited for my head to catch up. There was nothing much to see in the room. A wooden chair. Walls made of cinder blocks. An open door to a bathroom. A small table. No gorilla. Too bad. He was funny.

I didn't have any idea where I was. Or why. My brain started to spin, so I flopped back down. My pillow smelled like sweat.

I heard footsteps, followed by the swoosh of a bolt sliding free. I wasn't in any shape to deal with people. As the door opened, I shut my eyes and slumped deeper into the mattress.

A hand touched my shoulder, and then shook it.

"Come on, Eddie. It's time to play our game."

Game? What was he talking about? I tried to think. It was like jogging under water. Or under syrup. *Eddie.* That was me. Eddie Thalmayer. I knew who I was. But I had no idea who this guy was or why he wanted to play a game.

I wasn't going to do anything for him until I figured out what was happening. He shook my shoulder again. "Eddie . . . wake up. We have to move the marbles."

Vague images drifted through my mind. Marbles rolling across a table or floating above it. And, sometimes, wires stuck to my head. It wasn't a fun game.

The fingers tightened for a moment. My mind thought my shoulder should hurt, but my shoulder didn't seem to agree. The guy let go, and I heard him walk toward the door. "Those idiots must have overmedicated him again."

Overmedicated? Maybe I'd gotten sick or been in some kind of accident. But this didn't smell or feel like a hospital room. After the guy left, I opened my eyes and studied the wall next to the bed. A half-dozen large, black ants, as big as robins, swarmed over it. They were transparent. Except for their hula skirts. I blinked hard and the ants faded. I blinked again and they vanished.

I ran my tongue against my teeth and found a couple of crumbs. They were silent.

Overmedicated?

I'd been given something that turned my brain to fuzzy mush. Why? So I could play a game with marbles? No. There had to be more to it than just that. I dug through the mist, searching for something solid.

The answer jolted my numb body and sluggish brain. I knew why I'd been drugged and locked up. It was payback. I was here because I'd killed that man.

CONVERSATION BETWEEN PAMELA AND CORBIN THALMAYER DURING A CAB RIDE TO PHILADELPHIA INTERNATIONAL AIRPORT IN LATE MAY

PAMELA THALMAYER: I can't stop thinking about it.

CORBIN THALMAYER: It's hard. But sooner or later, you're going to have to let go.

PAMELA THALMAYER: It's my fault. I know it is. If only we'd paid more attention to Eddie. If only I'd been a better mother. We should never have let them send him to that school. That's where he learned to be a criminal.

CORBIN THALMAYER: It's not your fault. And it's not my fault. I thought the school was good for him. He seemed so much better when he came home. At least, at first. There's no way we could have known what was going on in his mind.

PAMELA THALMAYER: A mother should know. How could my son be capable of doing such an awful thing? How?

CORBIN THALMAYER: I don't know. I guess we'll never know.

*the glass marble game

THE MEMORY OF the murder was so brutal, I pushed it away. It couldn't be real. It had to be like the gorilla. Or the ants. But the gorilla and the ants happened here, in this room of rippling walls. The other thing—that awful, bloody moment—that was before. I searched my memories to see what else was before. It was like star-gazing on a cloudy night. I caught small glimmers. Flickering patches of light. I felt that if I could just clear my mind, the patches would grow together and make sense. I wanted to plunge my head into an ice-cold stream and shock away the fog.

As I lay there staring at the ceiling, the door flew open. "Good. You're awake."

He caught me by surprise. I started to look at him. But something in my gut warned me I shouldn't act alert. He thought I was overmedicated. But maybe I was undermedicated. My senses seemed clearer than before. I could feel an ache in my shoulder now—an ache that he'd caused. I turned my head toward him and then past the spot where he stood. Slowly, I let my eyes drift back, as if I was having trouble finding him.

Keeping my eyelids half shut, I scanned him for clues. His clothes didn't tell me anything. White shirt. Blue tie. Dark blue jacket with gold buttons. Gray pants held up by a thin black belt. Polished black shoes. One of his shoes smiled at me, but I was beginning to learn what to ignore. Shoes couldn't smile.

His hair was cut very short. His face had the sort of lines that came from a lifetime of scowling, but he was still a couple of years away from looking old. As my gaze flicked past his eyes, my stomach tightened like someone had jabbed me with a needle and injected poison into my gut.

A memory hit me. Years ago. There'd been a rabid dog in the street near the elementary school. The cops had shot it. All the kids went to see. They wouldn't let us get too close, but I saw his eyes. Dead, mad eyes. I'd had nightmares about those eyes for weeks afterward. That's what I was seeing now.

He looked like he was in shape. Not that I was planning to tackle him. The thought of violence brought back the image of the other man. And more memories. This guy—he'd been there, too.

I shuddered as the awful sound of snapping bones shot from the past, along with the scarlet splash of fresh blood. The snaps echoed and picked up the frantic rhythm of popcorn in the microwave. I gritted my teeth until the sound faded. I still didn't know for sure whether the memory was real. The moment floated in my mind, a single scene of fear and death, unconnected with anything else.

He slid the table over to the side of the bed. "Sit up."

I sat.

He moved a step closer. "Ready?"

I shrugged, not sure how alert he expected me to be. Should I mumble? Babble? Drool?

He placed a cardboard box on the table, flipped the lid open, and plucked out a clear glass marble. My gut clenched even tighter at the sight of it. He put the marble on the left edge of the table. Then he took out a paper target and set it on the right side of the table. The box was large enough to hold a lot more than one marble, but I couldn't see inside of it.

"Move the marble," he said. "Lift it."

I reached over to pick it up.

His hand shot out so fast I didn't have time to react. I struggled to hide my panic as he clamped his fingers around my wrist. "Not like that, Eddie. You know the game, right?"

I nodded, though I had no idea what he meant.

He relaxed his grip. I let my hand drop to my lap. *Not like that.* Then how?

Another glimmer burst through the clouds. Not just a star. A galaxy. An amazing, swirling galaxy with five dazzling constellations. I fought to keep my face slack as the memories flooded me. I understood, now. He wanted me to move the marble the special way. But that was a secret. Only five people knew about my hidden talent—my friends from Edgeview Alternative School. Their names were too deep in my heart to ever disappear behind the clouds. Martin, Cheater, Torchie, Lucky, and Flinch. Were they here, too? My heart beat faster at the thought. I wanted to see them. I desperately needed to see them. But I hoped they weren't locked up like me, doing tricks for . . . Bowdler. That's what the guys in the lab coats called him.

"Eddie."

I glanced up from the marble. "Huh?"

"You seem distracted. What's wrong?" Bowdler asked.

"Nothing."

"Who's Martin?"

I froze. I hadn't realized I'd spoken his name out loud. Had I mentioned the others, too? I needed to give Bowdler an answer. "My dog," I said, tossing out the first lie that came to mind. "Martin. He got shot. I miss him."

"I'm sure you do." He pointed to the marble. "But you're starting to displease me. Let's get back to the game."

I remembered more. A swirling blur, like a TV show I'd halfway watched ten years ago. The game. He'd make me move the marble onto the target. Over and over. Roll it, float it, bounce it. There'd been all sorts of marbles. Glass. Steel. Pure black carbon. Plastic. Ceramic. I'd moved them all. Then he put up barriers. A sheet of glass. A cloth handkerchief. Metal foil. I guess he was testing to see what kind of stuff could block my power. But I could reach through anything. Glass. Steel. Flesh . . .

There were other tests, too. Distractions. Headphones with loud music. Noise. Blindfolds. Flashing lights. Strong odors.

I shuddered again as I remembered the electric shocks tingling through my arm, or the time the room smelled like ammonia. Sometimes, they'd attached electrodes to my head and printed out long strips of paper. There were several people who helped set up the equipment. They left the room before I moved the marbles. But Bowdler—he was always there for the marbles, and for all the unpleasant moments.

So he knew I could move things with my mind. There was no reason to pretend I couldn't. If I did what he wanted, he'd leave, and then I'd have time to think.

Move the marble. No problem. I reached out toward it with my mind—just like someone would reach out with an invisible arm—except the arm is as long as I want, and there's no limit to how many I have. I can be an octopus, or a hundred-handed giant like the ones in the Greek myths. Anything I can move with my muscles, I can move with my mind. The marble wouldn't be a problem.

I reached out with my mind to lift the marble. But the marble didn't rise. It didn't even quiver. It lay there, as cold and silent as Bowdler. I clenched my teeth and tried again. Nothing. The air around me grew hot and damp. I wanted to try harder, but I didn't know how. I was afraid to look at him. Afraid to tell him I couldn't do it.

I stared at the marble and wondered whether I'd imagined everything. Maybe I didn't have any power. Maybe none of my memories were real.

Martin, Cheater, Flinch, Torchie, and Lucky—had I dreamed all of them up? Had I invented their psychic powers, along with my own?

I wasn't creative enough to do that. I could draw and I could paint. I was a pretty good artist. But I could never invent anything so amazing. Flinch could. Yeah, Flinch was creative enough to dream himself up. I'll bet there was even a fancy word for that—dreaming yourself up. If there was, Cheater would know it. He knew all sorts of trivia. But if Flinch wasn't real, how could he create himself?

Now I was definitely starting to sound crazy. Maybe that was the answer. Maybe I was just flat-out crazy.

"Excellent." Bowdler flashed a thin smile in my direction, then reached inside the cardboard box. I expected him to pull something out, but he just fiddled around for a moment, then said, "Try again."

This time, I had no trouble. I could feel my muscles unclench with relief as the marble rose. I floated it toward the target. But when it was halfway there, the marble dropped to the table.

I flinched as Bowdler pulled his hand from the box, expecting him to grab my wrist again. Instead, he scooped up the marble and the target, and put them away.

"Get some rest, my little puppet. Your real training is about to begin." Humming, he pressed his palm against a metal plate by the door. The bolt slid open and he left the room.

I inched back along the mattress until I was wedged in the corner and hugged my knees tight against my chest, trying to vanish inside myself. *This can't be happening.* I dug my nails into my leg. *It isn't real.* The pain, still dull and distant, was real enough.

This is happening.

I remembered something Cheater had said, back at Edgeview. I could picture us, sitting in Martin and Torchie's room.

"If they find out about us, bad things are gonna happen. People hate anyone who's different."

"Yeah. They could cut us up to figure out how we work," Lucky said.

"Or lock us in a room," Cheater said. "You know, use us for weapons. Or as spies."

"It's like a secret weapon," Lucky said. "It works best if nobody knows about it. We can't tell anyone."

Back then, I'd thought they were being paranoid. But someone had found out about my talent and locked me in a room. I hadn't been cut up so far, but I had no idea what they were planning. I'd give anything to be with the guys right now. Even if we all had to go back to Edgeview, where we'd been dumped like unwanted animals. Even there, among the bullies and the stink of despair.

The stink of despair? Fancy words for a kid who was recently hallucinating gorillas. I realized my mind was working better. Why wasn't I totally numbed by the drugs? Bowdler had said something about me getting too high a dose. That didn't explain how I felt. . . . Maybe this time they'd given me too low a dose. It didn't matter why I was coming out of the fog. All that mattered was that I wasn't drugged now. At least, not completely. I still felt dizzy. Stray sounds—clicks and whistles and hums—floated through my mind. If I stared at my hand, the lines of my fingerprints seemed to whirl and spin. But at least I knew it was an illusion.

I needed to get away before they gave me another dose. With my powers, and a clear head, it would be easy to slip out of here. If I could trust my powers. I'd had a hard time moving the marble. Maybe the medicine had something to do with that, or I'd been distracted by the flood of memories. Or maybe Bowdler just shook me up so much I couldn't think straight when he was around. I looked at the chair. That would be a good test. As I was about to slide it across the room, the door opened again and a guy in a lab coat came in. I think it was the same guy who'd brought me the sandwich. He was carrying a small tray. No food. All I saw was a paper cup.

"It's time for your medicine," he said, reaching for the cup.

*at that same moment . . .

TRASH. THE NAME slipped into Martin Anderson's mind like someone had shouted it from two blocks away. Martin glanced toward the living-room window. But he wasn't looking at the street. He was looking toward the past. The sadness lingered. But he couldn't think about that right now. Someone else was shouting, much closer. Too close, and far too familiar.

"Are you listening to me?" his father yelled.

Martin turned his attention back to his screaming parent. "Sure. It's my hobby. I love hearing you shout. I'm happy any time I can see your tonsils. Just like you're happy when your boss yells at you for messing up."

I gotta get out of here, he thought as the angry lecture resumed.

WILLIS DOBBS—"FLINCH" to his friends—paused in the middle of a sentence as the name flickered into his mind. *Trash.* Eddie's nickname at Edgeview. Flinch lowered the microphone and stared at the ancient tape recorder in front of him, watching the cassette reels turning.

"How can I be funny now?" he said out loud. He swallowed against the lump that swelled in his throat. *It still hurts.*

But the best comedy sprang from tragedy. He knew that. He took a deep breath, and continued practicing.

DENNIS "CHEATER" WOO had been staring in the mirror, trying to work on his bluffing face, when the name hit him hard. *Trash.* Cheater was used to thoughts invading his head—both his own and those of other people. Just the simple act of looking at a mirror filled his mind with everything from the basic principles of optics to trivia about *Through the Looking Glass.* But he wasn't used to thoughts arriving with the force of spoken words. He dropped the cards and blinked hard as he remembered his lost friend. *Trash.* It had all been so horrible. So senseless. So . . . stupid.

This was a dangerous world, full of violence and anger. He'd been inside far too many minds, and heard far too many angry thoughts, to believe otherwise. *Maybe I shouldn't go to the game.* He didn't know these kids. But he had to go. He had to prove he was the best.

PHILIP "TORCHIE" GRIEG was usually happy. Today, a rare frown crossed his lips. He paused in mid squeeze, letting the note from the accordion die in the air as he thought about his old friend. *Trash.*

Across the road, a stray dog stared at him, as if startled by the sudden silence.

"It's okay, pooch," he told it. He sighed, checked the dry

grass around him to make sure he hadn't accidentally set it on fire, then played a sad song.

THE VOICE WAS nearly lost among all the others. Dominic "Lucky" Calabrizi only noticed it because it was different. More urgent. More connected, somehow, to his life. Not hollow and masked by the medicated numbness that swaddled him like ten miles of bandages. Another voice was the last thing he needed. Even worse, this voice carried sad memories. *Trash.* He clamped his hands over his ears. It didn't help.

*medicine dropper

THERE WAS NO way I was going to swallow any more medicine. If my power was working, I could fling the chair at the guy and make a run for it, but I didn't know how many people were here, and I definitely didn't want to get shot in the back as I was racing down the hall.

I needed to get rid of him without raising any alarms. I had an idea, but my timing needed to be perfect. That wouldn't be easy, since I still felt like someone had whacked my head a couple times with a two-by-four.

As the guy stepped toward me, I pushed his toe down just the slightest bit so it caught the floor. It worked. When he stumbled forward, I tugged at the tray. Again, just the slightest bit. It all had to seem like an accident. When he tried to catch his balance and grab the medicine, I slid the cup toward his fingers. He swore as the cup bounced from his grip. The liquid spilled over the tray. A drop splashed on my lip. I licked it without thinking, then braced myself for the bitterness.

That was weird . . . it tasted like water.

Cursing, the man wiped his hand on his pants and

stomped toward the door. He pushed his palm against the plate and stepped out. There was no click from the bolt when the door closed behind him. I hoped he was annoyed enough that he didn't notice.

I kept my concentration on the bolt as I walked to the door. It was easier to hold it back than to try to figure out how to trigger the mechanism once it closed. I opened the door and peered out.

From what I could see, the place wasn't very big—just a short hall with a couple rooms on each side. No windows. It had the damp, musty smell of a basement. I heard the clink of someone grabbing a bottle from a room at the back of the hall. Probably the guy getting more medicine.

I raced up the stairs at the other end of the hall, trying to move silently. I stumbled once, but managed to catch myself. There were four open doorways on the first floor. I peeked into the closest one to make sure nobody was inside. It looked like some kind of lab with all sorts of electronics stuff. I dashed past it. The next room was an office, with file cabinets and desks. I wasn't going to stick around to examine anything—not when I could see the front door ahead of me.

"Hey!" The shout came from downstairs. I guessed the guy had gotten back with the medicine already.

I blew past the other two rooms, slipped outside, and braced myself for a blast of cold air. Though the sun was low in the sky, the weather was surprisingly warm. I blinked and looked around, feeling like a bear coming out of hibernation. But I wasn't at the mouth of a cave in the woods. I was in the middle of a city block. There were narrow two- and three-story houses in both directions. Across the street, I saw a couple small stores and a coffee shop. I could hear car horns in the distance, and an ambulance siren farther off.

The fresh air helped lift some of the fog in my head. I jumped down the three porch steps, landing on the sidewalk. I knew I had to get away from the house immediately. As my mind cleared, and the sting of impact spread across my bare feet, I realized something else. I was about to attract a lot more attention than I wanted. In my rush to escape, I'd made myself highly visible. I guess I'd been living in them so long, I didn't even think about the fact that I was wearing pajamas.

It was like one of those dreams you're really happy to wake from. I was on a city street in pajamas, running from a monster. But this wasn't a bad dream. It was a bad reality.

A scruffy guy in jeans and an Eagles t-shirt stared at me as he walked by. I started to hunch down, but that brought back another strong memory. For years, I'd shuffled through life like some sort of human turtle, trying to duck beneath the radar of the real world. I wasn't going to do that anymore. I glared at the guy. *Look, man, the only real difference between you and me is that you've got underwear. And it's probably not all that clean.* The instant I caught his eye, he quit staring and hurried off.

I didn't stop to enjoy my victory. I had to get away. As I headed for the corner, I tried to act like it was the most normal thing in the world to jog down the street in pajamas, but I could feel my face flushing. I checked over my shoulder just in time to see a door fly open. A little girl raced down the steps, followed by her mother.

Wrong house.

Tell that to my heart. It didn't matter. The lab door would open any second. I spun around the corner, ignoring the pain of city grit abrading my feet.

I hurried a couple more blocks, turning corners at random, expecting to hear shouts of pursuit at any instant. When people stared at me, I stared right back. But I wasn't planning to spend the rest of the day dressed like a sleepwalker. I needed clothes. Right now. Which meant I needed money.

I stopped walking and tried to think up a way to get some quick cash. I could beg. But who'd give me money looking like this? I didn't have anything I could sell. As I stood there, a guy bumped into me, jolting me out of my thoughts. I glared at him, but he didn't even look back.

Jerk. His wallet was jutting halfway out of his back pocket. The next thing I knew, it was sitting in my hand. I'd floated it over before I even realized what I was doing.

The wallet was bulging with cash. There was more than enough money to buy everything I needed. Instead of relief, the sight of the cash made me gag. I fought back the sour flood of nausea that burned my tongue. *What's happening to me?*

I caught up to the guy and tapped him on the shoulder. "Hey, Mister," I said as he turned toward me. "You dropped this." I thrust out the wallet.

He slapped his back pocket, then snatched the wallet out

of my hand. For an instant, he glared at me suspiciously, but then relief took over. "Thank you. Thank you so much." He reached in and pulled out a twenty. "Here, I want you to have a reward."

"You sure? I don't really deserve this." I stared at the money, afraid to touch it.

"Take it." He practically shoved the bill into my chest.

I took the money. My gut twitched, but didn't make a major protest. I looked down at the twenty-dollar bill in my hand. Like it or not, I knew how I was going to fund my shopping trip. I crossed the street and spotted another jutting wallet. *It's not stealing. I'm giving it right back.* That thought helped a bit.

"Why are you wearing pajamas?" the second guy asked as he handed me a reward.

"I'm going to a sleep over."

The third wallet was easier. I didn't feel great about getting money this way, but I only took wallets that were already in danger of getting snatched. So I guess I could say I was giving people a cheap lesson in protecting their valuables.

I thought about how Lucky got in trouble. He'd find wallets, keys, jewelry, and all sorts of other stuff. That was his hidden talent—he could hear lost things calling out to him. He tried to return them. After a while, everyone thought he was a thief. I wonder what he'd think if he could see me getting rewarded and thanked?

Nine wallets later, I had almost one hundred and fifty dollars. I looked around for a place that didn't have a NO SHOES, NO SHIRT, NO SERVICE sign. Finally, I found a thrift shop, where I bought pants, underwear, a t-shirt, and a cheap pair of sneakers. When the girl at the checkout stared at me, I shrugged and said, "I thought it was pajama day at school. Boy was I wrong." She gave me a *whatever* look.

I put the sneakers on right there, then changed in a Mc-Donald's bathroom and stuffed the pajamas into the trash can. Perfect. I could blend in and go anywhere now. I felt a bit less like I had a large, blinking arrow pointing down at me. But as I walked out of the bathroom, a guy in a dark blue suit rushed through the door and bumped into me. I screamed and jumped back, ready to run.

"Sorry, kid." He edged around me.

It's not him. Get a grip. I scurried out of there.

Based on the street names and the large number of Eagles shirts and Phillies caps I saw all around me, I figured out I was in Philadelphia. That was good. I only lived about twenty miles away. After hunting around for several blocks, I found a pay phone that wasn't broken. I checked my loose change from the clothing store. I had just enough coins to call home. I couldn't wait to hear Mom's voice. Or even Dad's. They'd tell me what was going on.

The phone rang and rang. The answering machine didn't even pick up the call. I tried Mom's cell numbers, but got an out-of-service message. I tried to dial Dad's number, but my hand was shaking too much to press the right buttons. I wedged the receiver against my ear with my shoulder, then steadied my left hand with my right and tried again.

Out of service? No way. That can't be right. Dad never leaves the house without his cell phone. He even takes it with him when he goes out to the back yard. I can see him, sitting by the gas grill, letting it ring. Once. Twice. He'd pick up on the third or fourth ring. "Never act too eager," he'd tell me. "Not if you want to come out on top."

I tried all three numbers again, just to make sure. The result was the same. Did they know where I was? I wasn't even sure how long I'd been gone, but it definitely wasn't winter anymore. I went to a corner newsstand and checked the date on the paper.

It was June sixteenth—a bit more than a month before my fifteenth birthday. Why did I keep thinking it was winter? I shuffled through my memory. I'd gotten out of Edgeview right before school ended last June. Then, in September, I'd started my freshman year at Sayerton High. The teachers were a bit weird around me at first, because of my reputation for breaking things. I suppose they expected trouble. But, thanks to Martin, I was no longer a victim of the telekinetic power that had nearly ruined my life and given me my nickname. Instead of letting my talent run wild, I was learning to do all sorts of things with it.

And I guess that was the problem. I'd played around too much. Someone had discovered my secret.

A police car cruised past. My instincts flipped. Run and hide? Chase after them and ask for help? I didn't think either of those was the right move.

I needed help. But until I knew who had kidnapped me, I didn't think I could trust anyone—except my friends from Edgeview. As I thought of them, I stared at the small, round scar in the center of my right palm.

Torchie would help me. Just like I'd do anything for him. But he wasn't great at figuring things out. Lucky was fiercely loyal, but he was also as tense and touchy as an unsprung mouse trap. Cheater was smart, but the stuff he knew didn't have anything to do with the real world. He could tell you who invented asphalt or why people drive on the right side of the road, but he never remembered to look both ways before he crossed the street. He was always bumping into trouble.

It had to be Martin or Flinch. Flinch was the smartest as far as the real world, and the funniest, but Martin had an awesome ability to solve problems, and to get people to work together. That's who I needed to talk to. If anyone could help me figure out what was going on, it was Martin.

He lived farther away, which meant the call would cost more. I figured I didn't have enough coins. I saw a bank on the next block. I headed there to get some change. When I saw my reflection in the window, more memories rushed back, kicking away the remaining drifts of fog from my brain with a jolt, and flooding my throat with another harsh wave of nausea. I remembered that single moment of greed and stupidity—the moment that led to all this.

E-MAIL FROM CHEATER, DATED FEBRUARY 17TH

From: TriviaKing@quickmail.net
To: Martin316@xmail.com,
          Dodgeboy@zipnet.com,
          PhilipGrieg@cheapmail.com
Subject: Not to be paranoid, but . . .

Have any of you guys heard from Lucky? He
hasn't texted me in a couple weeks. I
called his house. His dad took a message
and promised Lucky would call me back,
but he didn't. I don't want to call again
and make a pest of myself.

*sometimes, it's ok
to swear

I STAGGERED AWAY from the bank window as that one memory kicked loose a dozen others, each one freeing more in turn, like a nuclear fission reaction. The past returned with a blinding flash.

MARTIN HAD BEEN the first one to get out of Edgeview. I got out a couple weeks later, right before the end of the school year. So did Flinch. The other guys all went to summer programs so they could be allowed back in regular school in the fall.

But it was the day he left—the last day we were all together—that's important. We'd taken a vow. Martin had just finished cramming his stuff in his bag, but we still had an hour before he had to go.

"We can't ever tell anyone about our talents," Lucky had said. "It's too dangerous."

"What about our parents?" Cheater asked. "Or my big brother?"

Martin shook his head. "Not even them. Unless we absolutely have to."

"That's the way it's gotta be," Flinch said. "Normal kids get beaten down just for being a little different. Wear the wrong shirt, listen to the wrong music, and you get crushed. Imagine what would happen to us. We all need to swear not to tell anyone."

"Right," Martin said. "We don't tell. And we don't leave any evidence. We shouldn't even mention our powers when we email each other."

Torchie held up his little finger. "Pinky swear?"

"No way," Lucky said. "This is a blood oath. Hang on. . . ." He dashed off, then came back a moment later with a compass—the kind you use to draw a circle. He jabbed the point into his palm, then held out his hand.

"Do you know how many pathogens are in human blood?" Cheater asked.

"We'll count them later," Lucky said, jabbing Cheater with the compass.

The rest of us stuck ourselves, then clasped hands and swore to keep our talents secret from the world. I'd kept my vow and kept my mouth shut. But I also couldn't help testing my limits. I'd even found I could move stuff I saw through binoculars, or in a mirror, though not stuff I saw on live TV.

School definitely got better now that I had control of my power and wasn't snapping and breaking stuff all around me. Even with my control, I was reluctant at first to do anything. The memory of my punishment lingered.

But temptation always wins out over memory. At first, I played around with small stuff. I could make a biology specimen twitch just enough to get a whole table to scream, or open some lockers for fun. Then I discovered the thrill of being an anonymous hero.

I loved watching Max Eldretch, the nastiest kid in my class, suddenly trip and fall in the cafeteria—especially when he landed face-first in a trayful of nachos. The whole place laughed and clapped. Even though I couldn't take credit, I felt like they were applauding me.

But I didn't just punish the wicked. I also helped the weak. Like Aubrey Toth, the class nerd. I helped him hit a double in gym class. I can still remember his stunned expression when the ball shot over the heads of the outfielders. The pitcher was pretty shocked, too. And it was funny how my one mean teacher, Mr. Dinzmore, was always losing his pens.

Life at home got better, too, at first. Things had been tense between me and my parents for years. Mom kept trying to get inside my head and find out what was bothering me. Dad would glance up from his phone calls when I walked by, and study me like he was staring at a puzzle written in another language. I could hear them talking at night. The words were never clear, but the tone was unmistakable. *What did we do to deserve this? What can we do to fix it?*

There was a time, back when I was little, when Mom sang songs to me and took me on trips to the zoo. There was a time when I sat at the table after dinner and drew pictures of dragons while Dad told me about his business deals. I never understood what he said, but I loved that he said it to me.

I know the exact moment when my life took a sharp left turn. The memory still has the sting of a razor cut.

Fourth grade. Mr. Rostwick's class. The day we got back from spring vacation. The end of my life as a normal, happy kid. There was a new kid at the desk next to me. I don't even remember his name. Just that he was twice my size, with small, beady eyes and a crusty patch of dried snot next to his left nostril.

"Whatcha doing?" he asked before class started.

I held up the drawing I was working on. I'd always liked to draw. Especially monsters and rocket ships. This one was a cool monster with three heads.

"Can I have it?" he asked.

"Nope."

He reached over and snatched it. "It's mine now."

"Give it back."

He shook his head. "Finders, keepers."

I wanted to hit him, but Dad always told me not to solve problems with my fists. *You can negotiate with anyone.* "You didn't find it. You stole it." When I tried to grab it, the kid yelped like he'd been pinched, and leaned away from me.

"Edward! Stop bothering the new boy," Mr. Rostwick said.

"But he—"

"I said stop." Mr. Rostwick gave me the glare he used when he was about to explode.

I gave up. "Fine," I whispered. "Keep it." I figured I should be happy he liked it that much. But the kid stuck his tongue out at me and started to slowly tear up the drawing. As he ripped each piece off, he slipped it in his desk. I grabbed the legs of my desk and squeezed them hard to keep from leaping up and smashing him in the face.

When we headed out for recess, I went around the building and climbed back into the classroom through the window. I was just going to get the pieces back. That's all. And, okay, maybe tear up something of his.

Mr. Rostwick caught me right when I reached the kid's desk. "What are you doing?"

I froze. For a moment, I couldn't even remember how to breathe. Mr. Rostwick walked over and knelt so he could look into the desk. He gasped, and then started pulling stuff out and piling it on top of the desk. "Edward, how could you?" Everything was trashed. The notebooks were shredded, the pencils were snapped in half, and the calculator was pulled apart. It looked like someone had tossed a grenade in there.

"I didn't do it." I tried to think of some way to prove I was innocent, but my mind was as frozen as my body.

"Young man, you are in serious trouble," Mr. Rostwick said.

My parents had to come in for a conference. Nobody believed me when I said I hadn't done anything. They took money out of my allowance to pay for everything. Before the end of the school year, I'd gotten in trouble two more times— once for trashing another kid's desk, and once for destroying the set for the play after I wasn't allowed to help paint it. Nobody would believe I hadn't done either of those things. Mom and I had more and more long talks. Dad and I had more and more long silences.

It got worse in the fifth and sixth grades. Everyone started calling me Trash. Kids tried to get me mad, hoping they'd see me wreck something. Things got wrecked, but nobody ever saw it happen. By then, I had a permanent desk in detention, and no chance of an allowance for a very long time.

When I went to middle school, I hoped things would change. But the first week there, I got into an argument with my art teacher, Ms. Eberhardt. She wanted me to hold my pencil a different way. I told her I'd been holding it this way all my life. She snatched it out of my hand and broke it in half, then told me to get out of her class. I stomped out of there and left the building, but went and sat outside the window of the art room until long after school let out. I was too angry to go home right away.

I probably should have stayed away longer. That evening, the police showed up at our house. The entire art room had been trashed after school—except for my project. Every pencil, brush, and piece of pastel was broken. Every paint tube was squeezed empty and stomped flat. There wasn't a single whole sheet of paper left. All the easels were trashed, and both blackboards had been ripped from the walls. Even the lights had been broken.

The school pressed criminal charges. Dad wouldn't look at me during the hearing. Mom's face was so sad, I couldn't look at her. The thing is, they could have hired the best lawyer in the country. Mom wanted to, but Dad refused to help me. He said I needed to understand that all actions had consequences. I didn't have a chance. The judge gave my parents a choice—juvenile detention or Edgeview. At least they'd picked the one I was able to survive.

I can look back now at the trail of smashed and broken stuff, and understand how my parents felt. I think the worst part for them was that I'd never admit I'd done anything. The worst part for me was that they didn't believe me when I said I was innocent.

When I got home from Edgeview, it took Dad a while to even talk to me. But after I made it though the first marking period without any problems, and brought home a good report card, he started to relax and talk to me again, like he did when I was little. He'd explain the business deals he was doing, and I'd tell him how my classes were going.

I especially loved high-school art class. It wasn't just stupid craft projects like we'd done in elementary school. We learned about the golden section and studied famous artists. Ms. Vanderhoven was great. In November, when we started doing watercolors, she let me use one of her own brushes.

"Nice?" she asked as I laid out a thin line of cobalt blue.

"Yeah." I couldn't believe the difference between her brush and the cheap ones we used in class. Those worked little better than cotton swabs. With this one, I had total control of the paint. I blotted it out and tried a dry-brush stroke. I stared at the results, amazed I could paint that way. "Do they make these for oil paints, too?"

"Absolutely. They make wonderful paints, too. I've got an extra catalogue you can have."

When I asked Dad for some money to buy a good set of Winsor & Newton brushes—that's the brand Ms. Vanderhoven uses—and some tubes of paint, he reminded me that I was still in debt. "You aren't getting any art supplies until you pay off the money you owe for all the supplies you destroyed."

"But that's not fair. I've changed. I don't get in trouble anymore." I didn't see why I should still be punished for something I had done when I was so different than I am now.

"I'm glad you've changed. But that doesn't erase your responsibility. You can't just remove red ink from the balance sheet."

"I'm really good at art," I told him. "You should see what I can do with a set of those brushes."

"Artists starve," he said.

"Not good artists," I said.

The phone rang. "We'll talk about this later."

I could tell he wasn't going to change his mind. But I didn't give up. When it got near Christmas, I mentioned the brushes to Mom. I figured she'd understand. She had a degree in English and was working as a fact-checker at a publisher's before she met Dad. She still worked at home, part-time. Being around editors and writers a lot, she'd have to be familiar with creative passions. But all she'd said was, "We'll see."

I saw. I got clothes for Christmas. I pretended I was happy. I wanted to sulk, or shout, but I'd gotten used to the pleasures of a life without drama. So I didn't pitch a fit or break anything in my room. Instead, I tried to take the clothes back and exchange them for money. But Mom had charged everything, so the store would only give me credit.

I had a savings account with several hundred dollars in it. Way more than enough for the brushes, and a couple tubes of paint. But Dad wouldn't let me withdraw anything.

I got up early the next Saturday, went to the bank, and

told the teller, "I lost my ATM card, but I have my school photo ID."

"No problem." She smiled at me like she really understood. According to her name tag, she was Monica, and she was happy to help me with all my banking needs.

"Thanks." I felt a twinge of guilt, but it was washed away by the thought of those brushes. And a big tube of titanium white oil paint. Besides, it was sort of true that I'd lost the card. At least, I'd lost control of it.

"I'll be right back." She walked over to a file cabinet and pulled out a sheet of paper, then came back and handed it to me. "Here. Fill in all the information, and we'll mail a new card to your parents."

"To my parents?"

"That's the rule with custodial accounts."

Dad worked from home a lot. If he saw the letter in the mail before I could get my hands on it, he'd know what I was doing. "But I need the money now," I said.

She spread her hands and shrugged. "If it was up to me, I'd be happy to help you out. But we have to follow regulations." She leaned forward and whispered, "Banks can be a real pain to deal with." Then she smiled again, like she really was sorry.

I turned away. In the old days, I guess something would have gotten broken. But I was under control. As I started to walk out, I glanced over to my right and saw something that sent a rippling chill of excitement across my skin.

LETTER FROM TORCHIE TO TRASH, SENT THE PREVIOUS SUMMER

Dear Trash,

I'm in love. My Mom took me to Musikfest in Bethlehem, and I heard a whole band playing accordions. They are so awesome. I couldn't stop stomping my feet the whole time—at least, not until the musicians asked me to stop stomping so loudly. I need to get one. (Don't worry. I'm still playing the harmonica.) I figured that since you like art, you'd know what I mean. But they're expensive. So I've been saving up my money. You're lucky. All you need is cheap stuff like pencils and pens.

I got a paper route. It pays pretty good. or it would, except I have to replace the papers I burn. But I'm getting a lot better. I don't start nearly as many fires as I did before Martin helped me.

I hope you are having a good summer. Maybe you can come visit me sometime. I never get to see any of you guys. Wouldn't it be great if we could all get together?

Your pal,
Torchie

*moving violations

NORMALLY, I'M PRETTY sure you can't see inside a bank vault. They probably don't want customers staring at the money and getting crazy ideas. But there was a reflection in the glass of the window where the drive-through tellers sat. Not only could I see inside the vault, I could see stacks of bills on a cart.

I remembered a piece of the endless trivia Cheater had shared with me back at Edgeview. There was a famous bank robber. Willie Sutton. That was his name. After he was caught, they asked him why he robbed banks. He answered, "Because that's where the money is." I wasn't going to rob a bank. But I was going to get my money.

I walked over to the counter along the back wall where they have the deposit slips. I grabbed a pen and pretended to fill out the form the teller had given me. Still looking at the reflection, I pushed a stack of bills from the cart and let it fall to the floor. If anyone saw it happen, they'd pick up the bills. I waited a moment, then slid the money out of the vault and down the corridor to the lobby. It was so easy. I moved the bills along the side of the room, right where the wall met the floor. Nobody noticed. The customers in line were all staring straight ahead. The tellers were all busy with the customers.

Once the money was near me, I moved it over by my feet and up my leg, right into my hand. Then I jammed the stack in my pocket and strolled outside, trying not to rush away like a fleeing bank robber.

I didn't want to count the money in the street. I went next door to a bookstore, hoping I'd gotten enough for the brushes. It wasn't really stealing. Whatever I got, I'd just never withdraw that amount. I'd let it stay in my account forever. So—me and the bank—we'd be even.

I went over to the poetry aisle, which is never crowded, and pulled the bills from my pocket. Instead of Washington or Lincoln, I found myself face-to-face with Benjamin Franklin.

"Hundreds . . ." I said as the meaning of that sunk in. I didn't know how many bills were in the stack, but I was definitely holding a lot more money than I had in my account.

I'd just robbed a bank. Big time.

Then a thought hit me—I could walk home and nobody would ever know. It would be the perfect crime. The teller had never looked at my ID. Even if she had, there was no way to connect me to the vault. It might be weeks before they even realized any money was missing. A bank this size probably dealt with a hundred times that much cash every day. *I could keep the money.* It wouldn't matter if I never got another penny of my allowance. I could buy anything I wanted. Brushes, paints, a roll of canvas, and a stretcher.

Even some of those really expensive art books with the full-color illustrations.

But someone would get in trouble. I thought about the teller who had smiled at me. Monica. Someone at the bank—maybe her or one of her friends—would get blamed for the missing money. I knew what it felt like to be accused of stuff I hadn't done—at least, not done on purpose. As thrilling as it was to think about the perfect crime, and a fistful of brushes, I had to take the money back. It would be easy enough to float the stack to the vault.

It should have been easy—except when I got to the door, it wouldn't open. In my panic, I almost threw the bolt open with my mind. Then I took a look at the hours listed on the door. The bank closed early on Saturday.

Calm down. It's not a problem.

I saw a drawer next to the door for night deposits. It was locked, but my mind was the key. I unlocked the drawer and dropped the money inside, then took off. The money was back in the bank, even if it wasn't in the vault. That would have to be good enough. There'd be a mystery, but no real crime.

For the next three nights, I could hardly sleep. Every time someone came to the door, I figured it was the FBI. Every time the phone rang, I jumped. Every time the loudspeaker in school crackled, I expected to be called to the office, where I'd be met by the police and my parents. After a couple more days, I started to relax. After a week and a half, I stopped worrying and congratulated myself for pulling off the perfect non-crime.

The men in the dark blue suits showed up two weeks after

that. They were standing on the sidewalk when school let out. One of them had a photo in his hand. His hair was cut really short, like he was in the army. His dark-blue jacket had weird buttons with gold stars on them. The other guy was a bit older. His hair was slightly longer on the sides, but he was bald on top. His buttons were normal. They both looked like they belonged to some sort of serious organization. I figured they were narcs. I didn't think they had anything to do with me.

By the time they'd trailed me halfway home, I couldn't deny something was going on. I crossed the street. They followed me. Instead of turning right at the next corner, toward my house, I turned left, toward one of the older developments where the houses were crammed close together and narrow side streets twisted off in all directions. I figured I could lose them in an alley. But I guess they realized I was planning something, because they started to jog toward me.

I was about to run when one of the guys called out, "You can't get away, Eddie."

I spun around at the sound of my name. The older guy snatched the photo from the other one and held it up. Even from a distance, I could tell that the picture was a grainy black-and-white shot, like the kind they show on the news after someone robs a convenience store. It was probably taken from a security-camera video.

"We know who you are," the guy with the short hair said. "We know where you live. We know everything."

No way. Nobody knew everything. Except my friends. And they'd never break our vow. I pressed a finger against the scar in my palm. "I don't know what you're talking about," I shouted. "Leave me alone."

"You run now, you'll be running the rest of your life," the older guy said. "Is that what you want?"

"I want you to go away."

"That's not going to happen." He stopped about six feet from me. "We saw what you did. We don't care about the money. You aren't in trouble. So relax, okay? This isn't about the bank. We want to help you use your skills for everyone's benefit. Cooperate with us and everything will be fine. Right now, we just want to introduce ourselves." He took a step toward me.

I backed a step away. "I didn't do anything."

"You're too smart to believe that will work."

"Just leave me alone."

He shook his head. "It's far too late for that. Listen, young man, you can trust us. We're the good guys. USA all the way."

Just then, the guy with the short hair dove toward me. Flinch would have seen it coming, and Cheater would probably have realized what the guy was thinking. I didn't have that sort of warning, but I reacted quickly enough to save myself. While he was still in mid-air, I slammed him down at my feet. I can't lift a person very easily, but I can give someone a persuasive nudge when he's already moving.

"Wait," the older guy shouted. "Don't do anything stupid." He dropped the photo, reached one hand out toward me, and shoved the other inside his jacket.

That's when I snapped all of his ribs. I wasn't even thinking. I didn't plan to hurt him. The most sickening sound shot through the air, like a string of firecrackers. The guy dropped to his knees and his face went pale. He opened his mouth. I thought he was going to scream. Instead, he let out a wet moan as blood gushed from his mouth.

I wobbled back, sickened by what I had done. Something stung my neck. I looked down. The other guy, still on the ground, held a gun pointed at me.

I ripped the gun from his hand and sent it flying across the street. But the rushing darkness told me it was too late. I realized I'd already been shot.

"Sweet dreams," he said. "You and me—we're going to make history."

I tried to pull the dart from my neck. But my hand wouldn't cooperate. Neither would my mind. Then something flipped a switch in my brain and everything shut down.

AN INTERNAL FBI MEMO RECENTLY OBTAINED UNDER THE FREEDOM OF INFORMATION ACT

To: All field offices
Subject: Clarification of request from ███████████████

As covered in last month's briefing, we have been requested to forward to ███████████████ all material related to any cases marked "unexplained." Please note that this does not include instances where the perpetrator is merely unknown. ███████████████ has requested we provide reports of only those crimes where the means or method remains unexplained.

*a year before—a random act of meanness

"**I THINK YOU'RE** about to learn a harsh lesson," Major Douglas Bowdler whispered as he watched the little boy. He paused on the sidewalk and pretended to adjust the buttons of his jacket as he waited for his chance. Sure enough, the boy put the large box down on his lawn and went back inside the house.

"Careless," Bowdler said. That was the problem with the world. People were careless. They lacked discipline. Their minds were weak. Nobody took responsibility for anything.

Bowdler walked to the edge of the lawn, where it was bounded by a waist-high chain-link fence, and looked into the box. Toy soldiers. Hundreds of them, each no bigger than a child's thumb. Obviously, this was the boy's treasure. It was nice to see that young people still admired soldiers, even if they didn't understand discipline.

He was pleased that he'd been in the neighborhood. He was looking for a location for the lab. The place he'd just checked out wasn't right. Too close to other houses. Too many large windows. No basement. He'd had his doubts about the suburbs, but his partner, Thurston, had insisted on exploring various possibilities.

Bowdler was sure the city would provide better choices than these outlying areas. Everyone minded his own business in the city. Not that it really mattered, since the lab would never be used to contain a human subject. They were hunting for something that didn't exist. He wasn't troubled by this. They were being well paid. Even though the property wasn't right, the trip wasn't a total loss. Not now that he'd spotted a target of opportunity.

He scanned the perimeter in search of a way to dispose of the toys. There were always storm drains. But he found something much better. Traffic had backed up at the light. A concrete truck was right in front of him. *Perfect.* Bowdler hesitated for a fraction of a second as he imagined losing his own priceless collection of military relics. But sympathy was for losers and empathy was for the weak. And he would never be as careless as this boy. He leaned over the fence, snatched up the box, took five steps to the curb, flicked his wrist, and sent the toy soldiers into the slowly rotating muck of sand, gravel, and cement. Five more steps and he replaced the empty box.

He didn't bother to stay and observe what happened when the boy discovered that his treasures were missing. The immediate reaction—the wailing and crying—wasn't important. What counted was the lesson. The lost soldiers would make an impression. The boy would learn responsibility.

Maybe even grow up to be a soldier. It was possible to mold young minds into any shape one might desire.

Pleased that he'd made the world a better place, Bowdler walked back to where he'd parked his car.

OVERHEARD AT A CONSTRUCTION SITE LAST JUNE

GUY #1: Hey, what's that in the concrete?

GUY #2: Looks like some kinda plastic.

GUY #1: There's a bunch of it. Should we tell someone?

GUY #2: You want to pour the whole job again?

GUY #1: No way.

GUY #2: Me either. Besides, it ain't a problem.

GUY #1: Yeah. Once this stuff sets, nobody will ever know.

look it up

EVERY MEMORY AFTER that moment when I got shot in the neck was a fractured piece of a fever dream. Fragments and snatches. All in that same room I'd just escaped from. I pushed the past from my mind and turned my attention to my present problem. I couldn't face the bank. At first, the guy at the news stand wouldn't give me change. I finally got him to give me three dollars worth of coins for a five dollar bill.

When I got back to the phone, I called 411.

"What city?" the operator asked.

"Spencer." I was glad I remembered that.

"Name?"

"Martin Anderson."

"We have no listing for that name."

Shoot. I realized the phone wouldn't be listed under his name. "Are there any Andersons in Spencer?"

There was a pause. Then she said, "Thirty-five."

"Thanks."

As I started to hang up the phone, I heard another voice from behind me.

"Move the marble, Eddie."

I dropped the phone and spun around. The gorilla threw a shower of sparks in my face. "You're starting to displease me."

I blinked hard and he vanished, leaving behind the smell of cinnamon. Even though my head was clearer, I still wasn't completely a citizen of the real world. I needed to get off the street and rest for a little while. Somewhere safe. Somewhere quiet where I could think. And I needed information.

I knew my way around Philly well enough to find the library. It was just a couple blocks north, and then across Logan Circle. There were people at all the computers, but that wasn't a problem. I spotted one guy who was obviously just killing time playing an online game, so I pressed some random keys. Then I made the mouse stick on the mouse pad. After that, I pressed a couple more keys. I was just about to play with the monitor's brightness controls when the guy muttered something and walked away.

I slipped into the empty seat, pulled up a white-pages search site, and got a list of phone numbers for anyone named Anderson in Spencer. Then I did a similar search for the last names of my other Edgeview friends—Woo, Grieg, Dobbs, and Calabrizi. I tried Dad's name, too, just in case my parents had gotten a different phone number, but nothing came up.

It was dark by the time I left the library, which made me feel less like a target. I wasn't going to try to get any more change. I had way too many calls to make to be pumping a pocketful of quarters into the phone. So I swung into a corner store and bought a phone card. Then I went back to the pay phone and got busy. I called each Anderson on the list and had pretty much the same conversation.

"Hi, is Martin there?"

"Who?"

"Martin."

"I think you have a wrong number."

"Sorry."

About halfway down the list, calling a Richard Anderson, I got a different answer.

"Who wants to know?"

"I'm a friend of his. Is he there?"

"He's grounded. No calls."

"Can I leave a message?"

"I told you, he's grounded."

"Please? Can you just tell him that—"

The guy slammed the phone down before I could say anything more. At least I knew I'd found him. Maybe there was more than one kid named Martin Anderson in Spencer, but the man on the phone was such a jerk I figured that pretty much proved I had the right number. Martin rarely talked about his parents, but from the few things he'd let slip, I got the feeling he had a rough time with his dad.

So did I. But I didn't care if I had problems with my dad. I wanted to go home. I wanted to put on my own clothes—my own broken-in sneakers and my own worn-out sweatshirt from the Dali Art Museum. I wanted to sit on the couch in the living room and watch television, or pull apart the paper just for the comic section. I even wanted to hear Dad talk about his business deals, or listen to Mom make endless phone calls to raise money for her favorite charities.

I headed for 30th St. Station and caught a train to downtown Sayerton. It was just a couple blocks to my house from there. As I passed green lawns and flower gardens bathed in the whitewash of streetlights, I felt like a ghost, traveling streets I hadn't walked since last winter. It seemed wrong that the trees weren't bare and the wind wasn't icy. It seemed weird that the air didn't carry the heavy smell of burned firewood.

My parents must have thought I'd run away or something. I tried to imagine how they'd react when they saw me. Mom would cry and hug me so hard I wouldn't be able to breathe. Dad rarely let his feelings show. He was always doing huge business deals with people who didn't understand the real value of the companies they owned. It was sort of like playing poker, except the stakes were way higher and Dad was the only one who could see all the cards. He wouldn't act surprised when he saw me, but I was pretty sure he'd be happy.

I was half a block away from home when a car pulled to the curb across the street from my house. Nobody parks on the street around here. Everyone has a garage. And visitors park in the driveway.

"Idiot!" I smacked my fist against my leg.

Obviously, this was the first place I'd run to. I moved behind a tree and peeked out, hoping I was wrong. Maybe the guy in the car really was visiting someone. But he just sat there, looking at my house. I was pretty sure he wasn't one of the guys with the lab coats. That was bad. It meant Bowdler had other forces he could bring in to help with the hunt.

At least he hadn't spotted me yet. But I was trapped. I couldn't go in the front door. I couldn't even risk walking away. Once I moved out from behind the tree, he might notice me. I needed a distraction.

I glanced back the way I'd come. A dump truck loaded with gravel was rumbling down the street. All I had to do was reach out with my mind and yank the steering wheel hard to the driver's left. The truck would swerve and ram the car. That would definitely be a distraction. But the thought of someone getting crushed made me feel sick.

There was an easier solution. I jiggled the truck's steering wheel back and forth, just enough to get the driver's attention. He stopped right next to the car, hiding me from view. I turned and dashed back to the corner, walked around the block, and cut through the yard of the house behind us. I went to my back door and tapped on the glass. I wasn't sure whether my parents were there. But if they were, I didn't want to startle them by walking in.

There was no answer. I risked a louder knock. Still no answer. So I pulled the dead bolt with my mind, and went inside. "Mom?" I called. "Dad?"

Nothing.

I checked the house, making sure I didn't walk past the front windows. The drapes were half closed. That was a bad sign. Whenever we went on a trip, Mom would leave them that way. She didn't want them all the way open so people could see that nobody was home, or all the way closed, so people would know there was nobody home. So she left them half open. Dad and I both found that kind of a funny solution, but we kept our mouths shut.

My bedroom door was closed. All the way. I was afraid what I'd find behind the door. An empty room? I wasn't ready to face that. I headed down the hall and went to their bedroom. Their luggage was gone. So was a bunch of clothes. I searched for clues.

I didn't find out where they were, but I found out where I was supposed to be. The clipping was in Dad's desk drawer.

For the first time in my life, I understood what people meant when they said that their flesh crawled. I could feel my skin ripple as I read the article, like ghosts were running rakes across my body. According to the paper, Edward Kenneth Thalmayer, beloved son of Corbin and Pamela Thalmayer, had died last January. There was a small, private funeral.

Apparently, I'd died in a fiery car crash in late January. Police figured I was joy-riding. My body had been so badly burned that the local police had needed the help of a federal forensics lab to make a positive identification. I stared at the clipping for a while, feeling a numbness that went far deeper than the drug-induced stupor Bowdler had used to keep me under control. Death by itself was too weird to think about. My own death was beyond weird.

Oh man—my parents thought I was dead. I couldn't even imagine what they'd been through. My throat closed up as I pictured my mom dressed in black, standing in front of a coffin.

I kept hunting. There was no clue where they'd gone, except I couldn't find their passports. I guess they'd left the country. Maybe they needed to get away from all the memories here. As far as they knew, their only son was dead. Worse, I'd died in a senseless, stupid way.

As more funeral images flashed through my mind, I raised a bottle of perfume from my Mom's dresser and hurled it at the opposite wall with my mind. Before it could smash against the wall and shatter, I stopped it.

I sat on the edge of their bed until the anger faded enough so my whole body wasn't trembling. *Never act in anger.* Another of Dad's sayings. Whoever made up those sayings had never met Bowdler.

I needed to find out what I was dealing with. Whatever agency Bowdler worked for must be pretty powerful. They'd kidnapped me and faked my death. I had no idea what else they might do. I figured I shouldn't even try to e-mail Martin or Cheater or any of my friends. Stuff like that left too much of a trail. I didn't use the phone or even turn on my computer. They could be watching all of that. I really wanted to get in touch with Martin. But that would have to wait.

I also needed to catch my breath and calm down. I felt like I was on an amusement-park ride that spun in every direction at once. I was so tired the whole world seemed fuzzy. I decided to stay here tonight and sleep in my own bed.

When I went to the bathroom, I almost flipped on the light, but caught myself in time. That was the toughest part— watching every move I made. I wondered if that's what life was like for Flinch. I hoped not. It was exhausting. Cheater had shown us a trick once. Ask someone to write a sentence without dotting any i's or crossing any t's. It's almost impossible. We're all bound by thousands of habits.

Starving, I went to the kitchen, hoping there'd be something in the fridge. I unplugged it before I opened it, so the light wouldn't go on. But it was empty. I guess my folks had cleaned it out before they left. I found corn flakes in the cabinet. There wasn't any milk, but I didn't mind dry cereal.

It was strange moving through a darkened house. But at least I was home. Though it felt empty without my parents here.

Tomorrow, I'd figure out what to do. Tonight, I just wanted to lose myself in mindless sleep and hope I was tired enough so that the dreams of snapped ribs and flowing blood would stay away.

FROM CHEATER'S TRIVIA NOTEBOOK

I'd rather
be in
Philadelphia

This is supposed to be on W. C. Fields's grave. But it is apocryphal. Most people don't know that. They don't know what "apocryphal" means, either.

PART TWO

where it is seen that
trash isn't the only one
having an eventful wednesday

*cheater misplays the hand he's been dealt

"I'LL TAKE TWO." Cheater pulled the seven of clubs and the three of diamonds from his hand and slid them face-down toward the dealer. He was glad his nickname hadn't followed him from Edgeview. It would be tough to get anyone to play poker with a kid called *Cheater*. And it would be impossible if they knew he could hear their thoughts. But that wasn't a problem because these guys at the table—a group of older kids playing high-stakes dealer's choice—had no idea what they were facing.

He was also glad to be out of Edgeview. Now that he understood his talent, he was able to avoid trouble. Martin had shown him how. But his talents came with a price. Knowing what people thought—that was brutal. He still couldn't believe how much the smart kids hated each other. It was like an undeclared war among a dozen small countries. They all wanted to see each other crash and burn. Even the nicest kids had terrible thoughts. Cheater admitted he wasn't any different. Sometimes he'd think dreadful stuff, especially when the bigger kids pushed him around at school. But right now, the only thought in his mind was cleaning out these guys.

He got a nine and a three of spades. No help for his pair of kings, but it reduced the odds for the kid across the table who was probably trying for a spade flush. Things were looking good, even without another king. The player on his left was bluffing with queen high, and the player on his right was holding two jacks. The two guys farther away were harder to read—one kept thinking about spades, and the other had a high pair—but Cheater was pretty sure he had them beat.

Despite all his advantages, he knew he stunk at keeping his face from revealing his hand. He practiced every day, but it didn't make a difference. His opponents always folded when he got good cards, until he discovered the obvious solution. If he couldn't hide his excitement, he needed to be excited all the time. That was easy enough. He knew plenty of interesting facts. As long as he was enthusiastic about sharing them, he could conceal his reaction to his hand.

He pointed to a bowl of chips on the corner of the table. "Hey, did you know a Native American invented them? How's that for a cool fact? George Crumb. At least, that's what the stories say. Though the stories could be apocryphal. That's a great word. It's what you call a story that might not be true. Like Washington and the cherry tree. Anyhow, this one is probably true. It's pretty interesting. The guy was a cook up in New York State." Cheater chattered away about the origin of the potato chip while the dealer gathered the discards.

He was up enough to bet big. The bluffer folded, along with the player trying for a flush. The kid with jacks stayed in. So did the guy who was running the game—a senior named Fritz who'd somehow gotten a key to a room in a cheap motel where they could play all evening undisturbed. The place was only half a mile from Cheater's home, but the run-down neighborhood seemed half a universe away.

Nice pot. Cheater met Fritz's raise and bumped him the limit. If he won enough tonight, he'd be able to stake himself at one of the hold 'em games he'd heard about over in Philly. He really wanted to go to Philly, one way or another. All afternoon, he'd been thinking about it. *I could stay with Uncle Ray,* he thought.

"Let's see what you got," the kid with the jacks said.

"Beat this." Fritz laid out his hand. He had kings, too. But Cheater had kept an ace, which beat Fritz's ten.

"Close one," Cheater said as he reached for the pot.

"Too close." Fritz clamped his hand around Cheater's wrist.

"Hey, what are you talking about?"

"You've won every hand where you didn't fold," Fritz said.

Cheater shrugged. "Guess I'm lucky."

"Guess I'm lucky," Fritz said, mocking Cheater's voice. "Nobody is that lucky. You marked these cards."

Cheater's pulse sped up as the players' thoughts flooded his mind. They believed Fritz. None of them could accept the possibility of losing to a skinny little kid with glasses. Each person at the table knew he was the best poker player in the world.

"You brought the cards," Cheater said. "And you dealt that hand."

Fritz tightened his grip and yanked Cheater halfway

across the table, scattering the neatly stacked piles of chips. "How'd you do it?"

"I didn't do anything," Cheater said. He picked up a clear thought from Fritz. *It's the glasses.*

"These are just normal glasses." As the words tumbled out, Cheater realized his mistake. Nobody had mentioned the glasses out loud. Now, he'd given them a reason to be suspicious. His only hope was to prove his innocence. He pulled the glasses from his face and held them out. "See for yourself."

Fritz snatched the glasses from Cheater and stared through the lenses. "These aren't any kind of prescription." He dropped them on the floor. "You must be using them to cheat."

"I have a mild astigmatism," Cheater said. It was true— his glasses only made a tiny correction. But he felt he needed them. He used his eyes so much. He read constantly. His brother kidded him about it, calling him a book sucker. He wished his brother was here right now. Or his friends from Edgeview. He wished anybody was here besides these four angry poker players.

Fritz stomped down on the frames. "I guess we'll have to beat the truth out of you."

Cheater closed his eyes as more thoughts tumbled toward him, crackling with enthusiasm and anticipation. *Let's kick his butt.*

flinch prepares for battle

"**FOLKS, PLEASE WELCOME** Willis Dobbs."

Flinch stared out at the crowd as the applause came to an end. He loved the thrill of starting a set. He loved the applause. He loved the laughs. But he loved the combat most of all. At least, the verbal combat. He couldn't help clenching his teeth when he thought about other forms of combat. Last summer, right after he'd gotten out of Edgeview, he'd used his talent for a different type of battle. It hadn't been pretty.

There'd been a boxing program at the Rec League. His mom had fussed a bit when he'd asked permission, but she'd finally given in. He'd signed up, figuring his talent for seeing slightly into the future would make him unbeatable. Up until Edgeview, his talent had done nothing but get him in trouble. He interrupted his teachers whenever they talked to him, and seemed distracted and jumpy all the time. Everyone thought he was twitchy and weird, but all he'd been doing was reacting too soon. Now, he hoped to use his talent to fit in.

The first time he stepped into the ring to spar, he was matched up against a scrawny kid named Juan who lived right down the block from him. Juan was always walking around with his nose in a book. He reminded Flinch of Cheater.

"You trying to be tough?" Flinch had asked after they'd put on their gloves. He wanted to take slow, deep breaths, but his lungs wouldn't cooperate.

Juan grinned. "Sure. Why not. Just don't hurt me too much."

"No problem. I'm totally new at this, too. So don't hurt me, either."

"You've got a deal."

The bell rang. Buzzed with adrenaline, Flinch had side-stepped Juan's first awkward punch and thrown a counter-shot to the jaw that dropped him like he'd been zapped with a stun gun. Juan wasn't the only one stunned. The whole gym went silent as heads turned toward the ring.

Flinch had looked down at Juan lying there with his eyes rolled halfway back in his head. He waited to make sure Juan was okay. Then he climbed out of the ring. He felt like he'd just done something dirty and shameful.

"Hey," the trainer had called. "Where you going? You got the stuff, my man. I can make you a champ."

"Takin' my stuff elsewhere," Flinch said.

He'd tried baseball, basketball, and even fencing. He wanted to find something to help ease the stress of constantly keeping track of his actions. But there was no joy when you knew ahead of time exactly where a pitch would cross the plate. The first hit or two felt good. Pretty soon, it all started to feel cheap and easy. Worse, it got boring—like playing a game of cards when you could see everyone else's hand.

But there was joy now, because victory wasn't guaranteed. He lived and died not just by his hidden talent, but by his true talent. Flinch reached out and pulled the mike from the stand. Then he smiled at the crowd. *Bring it on,* he thought. *Give me your best shot.*

martin walks the walk

"DROP DEAD!"

The second he shouted those words, Martin knew he'd crossed a line. But there was nothing he could do about it. Life didn't come with a backspace key.

As his father shouted back, veins bulging in his head, Martin stormed to the front door.

"Martin. Don't go," his mom called.

"Let him go," his dad said. "Good riddance. Let him find out what it's like in the real world. He'll come crawling home soon enough."

"He's only fifteen," his mom said. "We're responsible for him."

"Nobody's responsible for him. And fifteen is plenty old enough for a dose of reality."

There was more, but Martin rushed off, still fueled by anger, and let the words fade into the distance. He couldn't believe what his dad had done. The phone had rung right after dinner. Martin reached for it, but his dad snatched the receiver and snarled, "Hello?" Then he frowned, glanced at Martin, and said, "Who wants to know?"

"Is it for me?" Martin asked.

His dad ignored him. "He's grounded. No calls." A second later, he shouted, "I told you, he's grounded." Then he slammed down the receiver.

"Who was it?" Martin asked.

"Nobody."

"You don't have the right to do that."

The rest of the discussion did not go well. A moment later, just like that, he was a runaway. He didn't even look back until he'd traveled half a block. No sign of his dad. His mom was on the porch, her hands clutching the railing while moths swooped at the light behind her. He hoped she at least wanted to chase after him. But it didn't matter what she wanted to do. She wouldn't step off the porch. His dad probably wouldn't even let her call the cops. *It doesn't matter to him that I'm underage. Doesn't matter if I keep walking and never come back.*

Martin looked ahead to where the sidewalk blended into the darkness. How perfect. Everything in front of him was murky. The world could come to an end a mile up the road, and he wouldn't have a clue until he got there and stepped off the edge of the earth.

That described his future, too. Everything ahead of him seemed to be shrouded in darkness. He checked his pockets to verify what he already knew—not a dime. Not anything. All he had with him was a ton of rage and a useless talent for getting people angry.

torchie makes
a joyful noise

"**MOM, CAN I** go to camp?" Torchie asked.

"Oh, I don't think that's such a good idea. Remember what happened the last time you went?"

"I'm a lot older now. And this isn't regular camp, so there aren't any tents to catch fire. This is accordion camp." Torchie pointed to the ad on the page next to the comics. "It's in Philadelphia."

His mom leaned over his shoulder. "Oh my, that's expensive."

"Yeah, I guess so." In his excitement, he hadn't noticed the price. "That's okay. I don't need to go." He enjoyed staying home, especially after having to live away from home when he was at Edgeview. And he liked keeping his mom company since his dad was on the road a lot driving his truck cross-country. But for some reason, he couldn't stop thinking about Philadelphia. It didn't matter. He knew his mom was right—the camp was too expensive. And he really didn't need music lessons. He was learning so much on his own. He could teach himself just about any instrument.

Torchie got up from the table and grabbed his accordion.

It was time to entertain the neighbors. That was his mom's idea. Torchie remembered when he'd gotten the accordion. He'd come home from school one day in April to find the huge box sitting on the porch. He'd carried it right to the living room and opened it as fast as he could. The accordion was way bigger than it had looked in the picture on eBay, and a lot shabbier, but that didn't matter. He gave it a squeeze. What a great sound. He started right out working on his favorite song. The accordion wasn't just big. It was also really heavy, which made him sweat, but he didn't mind. He sweated all the time, anyhow.

"Philip," his mom had called from the kitchen a half hour later.

"Yes, Mom? Want to hear a song? I've got 'Oh Susannah' almost figured out. At least, the first part of it." The absolute best thing was that, unlike the harmonica, he could sing along with the accordion. That meant he could make twice as much music at once.

"Not right now. But you know what I was thinking. I'll bet that your music would sound even nicer if you played it outdoors."

"Okay, Mom." Torchie carried his accordion outside. What a great idea. The sun seemed to be smiling at him, just waiting for a song.

He discovered he liked to stand in the yard near the kitchen so his mom could still enjoy the music. But she'd started keeping the window closed, even though the weather was getting warmer. When he asked her about it, she explained that she liked it really hot in the kitchen so it was easier to cook stuff.

To help her hear better, he moved closer to the window. That way, she wouldn't miss any of his music.

Soon after that, his mom had told him, "It doesn't seem right that I'm the only one enjoying this. Music is meant to be shared. I'll bet some of our neighbors would like to hear how well you're playing."

"That's a great idea." Torchie had gone up the street to Mrs. Muller's house. He knocked on her door and waited for her to come to the porch. Then he played his best song for her.

"Want to hear another?" he asked.

"Why, Philip, I think your music is so beautiful, you should share it with lots of people. I'd feel selfish if you just played for me."

So he'd gone to the next house on the block, and then the next. Everyone loved his music so much, they told him he really needed to share it with other people. Some of them even gave him rides to houses far down the road. People in Yertzville really did love their neighbors and look out for them.

As far as Torchie could tell, they also traveled quite a bit. A lot of folks didn't seem to be home when he knocked, even if their lights were on and their cars were in the driveway. It didn't matter. Torchie was even happy playing for himself.

lucky has left the building

"PHILLY," LUCKY SAID.

"What?" the nurse asked.

"I gotta go to Philadelphia," Lucky told her. He hated cities. There was lost stuff all over the place, calling out to him. Walking down a city street was like sticking his head into a room with a thousand televisions. But it didn't matter how much he hated cities. He had to go to Philadelphia. That was the strongest voice. The one that almost drowned out all the others. That was the voice that knew him.

"Easy there," the nurse said, smiling at him as she held out his medicine.

Lucky gulped down the pills, not even bothering with water, then fell back on the bed as the wonderful numbness flowed through his mind, smothering all of the voices. They were still there, but they didn't seem to matter.

"Lucky," they whispered, calling him by a nickname that was pathetically inaccurate. He'd never had any real luck, except for meeting the guys. Thanks to them, a normal life had seemed possible after he'd left Edgeview. As he drifted into the comfort of nothingness, he saw the moment when it had all come apart.

At first, school hadn't been bad. He did okay in his classes and even made a couple friends. He thought he'd escaped his past. Until early last February, when they'd moved to the new building. That's when it all went horribly wrong.

As the door to his room closed, he heard the nurse say, "Doctor, I think we've made a breakthrough. He talked to me. He actually made sense."

"That's encouraging. What did he say?"

"He wants to go to Philadelphia."

*cheater discovers that poker is a contact sport

THE FIRST PUNCH knocked Cheater to the floor. Flashes of pain mixed in his mind with flashes of panic and scattered fragments of the laws of motion. Good old Newtonian physics. Equal and opposite reactions. A body at rest. His face had been at rest, and resisted the impulse to move, but the force of the fist had overcome inertia. His brain, inside his skull, had also been reluctant to move, even after his skull had shifted its spatial location. His brain had no choice but to follow. *Do thoughts have inertia?* he wondered.

A kick caught him in the middle of his back, right under the shoulder blades. More laws burst into his mind—force equals mass times acceleration. A heavy boot has more mass than a shoe. A fast jab has more acceleration than a looping hook. A whole lot of force was coming his way.

Cheater curled into a ball and tried to protect himself. A sphere had the least surface area of any geometric solid. But any surface at all was far too much right now. Thoughts rained on him, too, along with the punches and kicks. They hated him for a thousand reasons. He was smart, he talked too much, he looked different, and he was cleaning them out at a game they thought they were good at. They even hated him because he was short.

Something stomped down hard on his side. He let out a whimper, but clamped his teeth together. He knew anything he said would just provide more fuel for their rage.

After the next kick rocked his head, the sharp pains faded, replaced by numbness. He heard a conversation from far away.

"Oh great, I think you killed him."

"No way. He's still breathing. We'd better get out of here."

"What if he tells on us?"

"You're right. Maybe we should make sure he can't talk."

"Why bother? It would be his word against ours. Nobody would believe him. We can say we were at a movie or something. Let's just get out of here."

Cheater waited, not really caring what they did next. Though he was curious what they would decide. It was an interesting ethical problem. Commit a greater crime to eliminate the risk of being accused of a lesser crime? Maybe he could solve it using a game-theory matrix. First, he'd have to quantify the parameters . . .

He was still thinking about situational ethics when he passed out.

flinch kills his audience

"**THANK YOU. IT'S** good to be here." Flinch scanned the crowd, wondering who'd be the first to take a shot at him. Probably someone at the table in the second row that was filled with college kids. *I'll find out soon enough.*

This was his first time at The Laughing Gherkin—one of dozens of comedy clubs in the area that filled their evenings with local acts. The clubs were all the same—small spaces jammed with tiny tables charging large prices for miniature beverages.

He took a deep breath and launched into his routine. Before he could get two words out, a guy in the rear shouted, "Why don't you come back when you're old enough to shave?"

The instant the last word cleared the heckler's mouth, Flinch shot back at him with, "I'm old enough to shave right now." He jammed his hand in his pocket, gave the guy an exaggerated glare, and added, "Come on up and I'll shave a bunch of years off your life."

The crowd loved it. Flinch knew it wasn't the best comeback in the world. Even as he spoke, several better ones popped into his mind. *Yeah, I don't need to shave, but you really need to bathe. Why don't you go home until they find a cure for ugly?* But it didn't matter if the line wasn't the best. Not when it was the fastest. His mind was already fast. He could almost always come up with a good line to cut down a heckler. His brain was wired for comedy. That was his gift. His true talent. But his other talent—his supernatural one—gave him an edge no other comedian had. He really was faster than lightning.

Flinch waited for the perfect moment, just long enough so his comeback still lingered in the air, and not so long that his next words would seem like an afterthought. "Sorry, man. I saw *that* coming."

I saw that *coming.* It was quickly becoming his catch phrase. The sweet part was that he really had seen it coming. Heard it, too.

He picked up where he'd left off and finished the first joke of his routine. "As I was saying, I'm glad school's out. I had to take the bus. That's fine, except they use the same bus for the kindergarten kids. You know, there's only one difference between a kindergarten bus seat and a cat litter box." He paused a second, then hit them with the punch line. "The litter box is a lot dryer."

That went over nicely. As the laughs faded, a woman in the second row took a shot at him.

Flinch destroyed her before the last word left her lips. The crowd loved it. Even the woman had to smile. That's why she was there. That's why they were all there. Not just to hear his comedy routine. They were here for the dazzling comebacks.

He remembered reading about an old magic act where the guy caught a bullet in his teeth. People flocked to see him. Flinch knew they weren't just coming to see the trick—they were coming because, just maybe, they'd see the magician get shot. Which, sadly, eventually happened. The guy died on stage. *They won't see me get shot,* he thought. No way he'd die on stage. He'd already dodged the first two rounds and was feeling bulletproof.

"Sorry, lady," he said to his latest victim. This time, he paused for slightly longer, allowing the audience to pick up on the phrase. They all joined him, shouting out the words, "I saw *that* coming."

The whole crowd was into it, smiling like they were members of a special club. Flinch couldn't help grinning, too. But he was grinning for another reason. Here he was, getting all this attention for doing the very same thing that had gotten his pal Martin in so much trouble.

Me and my smart mouth, Flinch thought. Of course, his cuts were meant to be funny. Martin's were meant to hurt. But this was no time to think about his friends. Right now, he had to keep his mind on the crowd. A guy in the front row was rattling off an insult.

Loving every second of it, Flinch shot back and sliced him to ribbons.

I saw that *coming.*

*martin engineers
an escape

THE FIRST THREE blocks he walked, Martin mostly thought about strangling his father. The fourth block, he had brief fantasies involving explosives and a chain saw. The next two blocks, he thought about their argument and wondered if he'd overreacted. The block after that, he almost turned back.

But the thought of his father's mocking voice was enough to keep him moving. *I knew you'd come crawling home.* Martin couldn't give him that kind of ammunition. At the very least, he needed to stay away for a couple days, just to prove he could survive on his own. He'd made some friends at school, but they weren't around right now. His sister was working at a summer camp, but that was way up in Maine. If he wanted to avoid sleeping in the park, he had to go see one of his Edgeview friends.

Or I could go to Philly.

No, there was no reason to go there. It was odd he'd even thought of it. None of his friends lived in the city. His best bet was to visit Cheater. He was the closest—only about thirty miles away.

Good plan. But all his cash was back at the house, so he couldn't take a bus.

Something will come up. Whatever else Martin could say about his life, it was never uninteresting. He walked into town. Nothing came up, so he walked through town.

One mile down, twenty-nine to go, he thought. But a block later, he spotted two guys loading boxes and bags into a beat-up old Tercel. He moved close enough to peer into their hidden places and make sure neither was deeply ashamed— or deeply proud—of being an axe murderer or pervert.

"Got any extra room?" he asked.

One of the guys nodded. "Where you going?"

Martin told him.

"We can take you part way," the guy said.

"Good enough." Martin slid into the back seat. The two guys got in front. Martin knew the driver was proud he was pulling a 4.0 grade average in a tough engineering program. On the other hand, he was ashamed that he was cheating on his girl friend.

"Heading to school?" Martin asked.

The driver nodded. "Yeah. We're doing summer session at UD. We just came home for the day to get some stuff for the house we're renting."

"Delaware's great," Martin said. He took a deep breath, and convinced himself there was nothing sleazy about making them like him. That was the flip side of his talent. If he dug at someone's deepest shames and failings, he made enemies. If he stroked their deepest prides, he made friends. "I'd love to go there for engineering." It was a harmless lie.

And there could even be a bit of truth in it—if he had a clue what engineering students studied.

"No kidding?" The two guys exchanged glances. "That's our major."

"Cool." Martin settled into the seat. Riding definitely beat walking. He couldn't wait to get his license.

"You know what?" the other guy said. "We were going to head down 476, but if we take the back way, we can get you a lot closer to where you're going."

The driver nodded. "That's the least we can do for a future engineer."

"Thanks." Martin glanced out the rear window as the car pulled away from the curb. An hour ago, he'd had no idea what would happen to him. Now, he was headed where he wanted. Maybe running away from home wouldn't be all that hard.

torchie learns that wishes do come true

"**THANKS FOR THE** ride, Mr. Wickman," Torchie said as he got out of the pickup truck. He sure had the nicest neighbors in the world. They all loved his music. He grabbed his accordion from the back. He'd tried to bring it in front so he could play as they rode, but Mr. Wickman told him there was a state law against playing live music in moving vehicles.

"Did you have a good day?" his mom asked when he walked in the house.

"It was great. I figured out a new song." He started to play "Roll Out the Barrel."

"That reminds me," his mom said, "I signed you up for accordion camp."

"Really? I thought it was too expensive."

"Money isn't important when you have so much love for music," his mom said. "You need to make use of your gift."

"It's two whole weeks," Torchie said. "Won't you miss me?"

"Of course I will," his mom said. "But it's too good an opportunity to pass up."

"This is great. Are you sure we can afford it?"

"I'm positive. We had help. The neighbors are all so proud

of you, they chipped in money to help send you away. They said no amount was too much to pay to get you there."

"Can I go there right away?" Torchie asked.

"They already started this session. You'll have to wait for the next one. It's only two weeks."

"Ask them if I can start tomorrow, okay? I don't mind if I missed the first couple days."

"If that's what you want," his mom said. "I guess I can check with them."

"That's what I want," Torchie said. He couldn't wait to get to Philadelphia.

lucky dwells on the past

THE MEMORIES WEREN'T bad when they were wrapped in the haze. Lucky drifted and looked back. School had been okay. His talent was always there—he heard lost objects crying out—but it was under control most of the time. There wasn't all that much lost stuff around him. Just pens, coins, junk like that.

Martin had taught him to search for new ways to solve problems. Lucky's problem was simple. If he didn't pick up on the lost objects, their cries grew louder and louder, until they drowned everything else out. Once he took them, he had to keep them or give them away. It seemed like they needed to be owned. He wasn't even sure whether the voice was from the object itself, or some sort of imprint left by the owner. In his darkest moments, he wondered whether his only talent was to sense the objects. Maybe it was his own mind that spoke for them. The source didn't matter. What mattered was silencing the voices.

After two months in high school, and after filling three large cardboard boxes with the things he'd found, Lucky sorted the contents and gave them all away. He took pens, pencils, erasers, and markers to a local day-care center. He took the rest of the stuff to the Goodwill store. The people were happy to get the items. The voices remained silent. And Lucky enjoyed giving things away.

The two times he found a wallet, he took them to the lost-and-found departments of local stores. He knew better than to turn in anything valuable at school. That's what had gotten him into trouble in the past. You can only hand over so many wallets before people start to think you're a crook.

But there were plenty of stores and other places with lost-and-found departments, so that wouldn't be a problem. He was nervous the whole time he had each wallet with him—especially the one that had been cleaned out of cash—but he'd managed to take care of them without getting in trouble. It looked like his days of being called a thief were over.

Then, last February, because of overcrowding at his high school, the ninth graders had been moved to the new middle school. The instant Lucky walked in, he heard faint whispers. They seemed far off. But there were dozens of voices. Maybe even hundreds.

Between classes, he searched the halls, trying to find lost objects. There was nothing. The building was brand new. But the voices grew louder every day. Whispers became cries, and then shouts. He found a nickel, two pencils, and a pen. But none of that made a difference. By the third day in school, the noise became a distraction. By the fifth, it had become unbearable. He couldn't concentrate in class. People stared at him like he was crazy. He hated that more than anything. He tried to stay home, but his parents made him go to school.

The worst voices seemed to rise up from the floor. In the middle of shop class on Tuesday afternoon, Lucky couldn't take any more. Even the shriek of two lathes and a table saw couldn't drown out the voices.

He grabbed a hammer from the wall rack, knelt above one of the spots where the voices rose, and started smashing the floor. Chips of concrete flew up in his face. He felt a slash of pain as a fragment cut his cheek, but that didn't matter.

He kept hammering. The shop teacher shouted at him to stop. But Lucky didn't care. The teacher was just one voice among many. Too many.

He struck harder. The concrete cracked and crumbled. Something small and green jutted out from one of the fractures. With shaking fingers, Lucky grabbed it. A toy soldier. A stupid plastic toy, no bigger than the first joint of his little finger. He dropped it in his pocket, silencing it. One less voice in the hundreds that filled his head. He kept hammering and found another soldier in the concrete. Lucky realized they were spread through the school, calling out to him from everywhere. There'd never be silence until he got them all. Why had they done this to him? Who would have buried all those soldiers?

He'd have to break up every inch of concrete in the school. It would take forever. He didn't care. He knew he could keep hammering forever if he had to. He raised the hammer and smashed it down. Raised and smashed, again and again. There was more shouting around him. Lucky was shouting, too. Crying out with each blow. Swearing at the voices. Swearing at the idiot who had strewn lost objects into every square yard of the school. His throat was sore from shouting. His cries became hoarse barks. Sweat spilled down his face, mixing with the blood on his cheek. The wound burned, but he didn't care.

Someone grabbed his wrist. They tore the hammer from his hands, though he tried to hold on. He struggled to grab it back. It was the only thing that could save him. People pushed him to the floor. He screamed and fought. He kicked and thrashed. There was a sting in his arm.

And then peace.

flinch dwells on the future

WHEN HIS SET ended, Flinch headed to the oversized closet they called a dressing room.

"Willis?" a man standing between him and the door asked. He was wearing a very nice suit—expensive, but not flashy.

Flinch nodded, but kept his distance. He'd never had trouble after a set, no matter how badly he ripped anyone up, but he'd heard stories about comedians running into some hothead from the audience who took an insult too personally.

The man reached inside his sport coat. Flinch relaxed as he saw ahead of time that the man was only pulling out a business card.

"I'm Don Mackeson," the guy said as Flinch took the card.

"Whoa!" Flinch knew it wasn't cool to act surprised, but according to the card, he was face to face with a talent coordinator for "Standup After Midnight," a late-night cable show. "You offering me an audition?"

"Nope. You just had your audition. I caught your act. Very nice. You're a bit unpolished, in a charming sort of way, but we like fresh talent on the show. And you have a lot of potential. We're running a series featuring new faces. One of the acts had to drop out at the last minute. How old are you?"

"Fifteen." Flinch's head was spinning.

"Excellent. We'll need your parents' permission. And you'll need a chaperone. But it'll be a blast. We'll send a limo. Put you up in a fine hotel. Treat you like a king. What do you say?"

"You bet."

"Fantastic. We're shooting this weekend at clubs in New York, Hartford, and Baltimore. You get your choice."

New York. That was the big time for standup comics. There and Los Angeles, of course. And Chicago for improv. But to Flinch's surprise, he found himself asking, "Are you doing anything in Philly?"

"We're at a club there tomorrow. But it's kind of short notice. You ready to dive right in like that?"

"Yeah. I was born ready. Can you make it happen?"

"I can make anything happen. Pack your bags tonight. Call my office first thing tomorrow and we'll work out the details."

Flinch laughed as Don Mackeson walked away.

"What's so funny?" he asked, looking back over his shoulder.

Even now, still stunned and deep into day dreams of stardom, Flinch waited just a fraction of a second before speaking so his reply would have the perfect timing. "I never saw *that* coming."

*martin dwells on a box

"**YOU'D THINK A** couple of engineering students would be smart enough to keep their gas tank filled," Martin muttered. He couldn't believe the nightmare he'd been through.

They hadn't gone more than five miles when the car ran out of gas on some side road in the middle of nowhere. Neither of the guys had remembered to charge his cell phone. After arguing for ten minutes about the best way to go, the two of them took off to look for a gas station. Martin waited. He waited some more. He didn't have a watch, so he couldn't tell how much time had passed, but it seemed like a couple hours. Finally, he decided to start walking.

As he walked, he couldn't help reliving a day that was even darker. "I still can't believe it." It had been so horrible. And so sudden. He could remember every detail of that frozen morning in January when he'd learned the news about Trash. Of all of them, Trash had the most awesome power—the greatest potential of all. And he'd thrown it away for a joy ride. Martin had the newspaper clipping in his room. He didn't like to look at it, but he couldn't bear to throw it away. That was absolutely the worst day of his life. So far.

Eventually, he reached a small town. Everything was closed. The clock in front of a bank flashed the news that it was 12:14. After wandering around for another half hour, Martin decided the best place to sleep would be in a narrow alley next to a shoe store. There were a bunch of empty cardboard boxes piled in a Dumpster. Martin spread them out and drifted through the night until the sound of morning traffic woke him.

He staggered out of the alley, stiff from sleeping on collapsed boxes, wishing he could brush his teeth. He smoothed back his hair and looked around, not quite sure where he was.

Drop dead . . .

"Oh yeah," he said as yesterday's highlight reel played through his head.

He wandered a couple blocks, and then saw a green sign with an arrow pointing to the left. SAYERTON 8 MILES.

Martin stared at the sign as if it were a magical relic. *Sayerton.* That was where Trash lived. He wouldn't be there, but his parents would. Martin figured they might even let him stay overnight. Or feed him. Either way, it would break up his trip to Cheater's house.

Maybe he could catch another ride. Even if he had to walk, it wouldn't take that long. *Four miles an hour,* Martin thought. That was how fast people walked.

Or I can go back home.

No way. Not yet. If he came back so soon, looking like a scruffy stray cat after less than a full day on his own, he'd never hear the end of it from his dad. There was no choice. Right now, he was on a one-way road.

A CONVERSATION BETWEEN
MR. CALABRIZI AND DR. KELNER

DR. KELNER: I really think it might help us get
through to him.

MR. CALABRIZI: But why Philadelphia?

DR. KELNER: We don't know. It must have some
special meaning for him. That doesn't matter right
now. I just think if we move him, we may see some
progress.

MR. CALABRIZI: Sure, if you think it will help. We
have to try it. I don't see how it can make things
any worse.

PART THREE

which covers a
thursday that makes
wednesday seem like a day of rest

there and back again

BOWDLER WAS INJECTING something into my arm. I couldn't move. I couldn't breathe. He put a tube down my throat that pumped air into my lungs and then sucked it back out. The tube kept me alive, but made me wish I was dead.

"Move the marble, Eddie."

I woke up screaming, amazed that my paralyzed body could fling itself out of bed. As my cries echoed against the bedroom walls, I realized where I was and crawled to the window to make sure the sound of my terror hadn't reached outside. A strange car was still parked at the curb across the street. I held my breath and waited, but the door of the black sedan remained shut.

The dream had been awful. But the worst part was that my mind hadn't invented anything. This wasn't a random dream. This was a memory. For one of his tests, Bowdler had injected me with something that paralyzed my muscles. My heart could still beat, but my limbs froze and my lungs didn't work.

"Move the marble, Eddie." His dead-dog eyes showed no emotion as he hovered over me, one hand on the tube that was keeping me alive. Unable to blink, unable to twitch a single finger, I floated the marble for him.

I'd escaped the dream by waking up. I had no idea how I could escape the memory. Except by thinking about other, worse memories. I backed away from the curtain, sat on the floor beneath the window, and tried to figure out what to do.

Who are they?

Bowdler had a photo from the bank video. That's the sort of thing the FBI would have. But the FBI doesn't kidnap citizens and fake their deaths. I think I'd heard someone call him "Major," once. The lab didn't look like it belonged to the army. But Bowdler's haircut, and the way he moved, made me think of a soldier. Whatever organization he belonged to, I'd probably never heard of it. Maybe nobody had heard of it.

There was only one place I'd find any answers. It was the last place I wanted to go, but I had no choice. I didn't know where my parents were. I didn't know who I could trust. And I was afraid it wasn't safe to get in touch with any of my friends. I had to go back to the lab. But I'd be far from paralyzed this time. And if Bowdler crossed my path, I wouldn't be the one who'd be helpless.

The thought of all he had done to me collided in my mind with all the things I could do to him. The fury of the images made my heart race. Nobody messes with my family.

I filled a backpack with some clothes, my toothbrush, and a couple paperbacks. I wasn't sure how long I'd be away. I slipped my MP3 player into my pants pocket. I didn't take my good one, but I had a cheap shuffle-play one that was pretty rugged. My parents usually kept cash in the bedroom.

It was weird how I felt a twinge of guilt when I opened Mom's jewelry box and lifted out the top compartment. I found about seven hundred dollars in the bottom, which I jammed in my pocket.

I didn't bother with the cereal since I knew I could get a good breakfast in Philly.

When I peeked out the front window to get a better look at whoever was parked there, I saw the car had a different guy in it. This guy was definitely bigger than the guy I'd spotted last night. He barely fit behind the wheel. So Bowdler had more manpower. Which meant more bad news for me.

A yellow bus rolled past the house. Even through the closed window, I could hear the kids singing a song. Lucky them. Nothing to worry about. Nothing to fear. On their way to a camp or something.

I slipped out the back and cut through a neighbor's yard. When I got near the train station, my paranoia started to kick into high gear. Last night, the car had just pulled up across from my house when I was half a block away. Maybe other people had been sent to look for me, too, and they'd just missed me at the station. That might mean there was someone there now, waiting for me to get off a train. The boarding platforms were up a flight of stairs. I bought a ticket from a vending machine at the bottom of the steps, then moved up just high enough so I could check across the tracks where the trains from Philly stopped.

I spotted a guy in a dark-blue suit, with buzz-cut hair, sitting on a bench, staring down the tracks toward Philly. Maybe he was waiting for the train. Or maybe he was waiting for me.

As the approaching train blasted its whistle, he glanced at something he held cupped in his right hand. My picture? I moved back down the steps and waited. The train from Philly arrived. When it left, I checked again. The guy was still sitting there.

At least there wasn't anybody on my side of the tracks. Nobody was looking for me to sneak back into Philly. They were all trying to catch me sneaking away. I kept out of sight and waited until my train pulled up, then dashed onto it and rode back to 30th St. Station.

It was late morning when I reached Philly. There were more men in suits watching the departures. I hunkered down and stayed in the middle of the crowd leaving the station. After I crossed the street, I ducked into the first alley I came to, made sure nobody was watching, and floated my backpack up to a rooftop so I wouldn't have to carry it with me all day. I kept one paperback, because I had a feeling I'd need to kill some time.

I backtracked until I found the block where the lab was. I watched the lab's door from the corner for a while before going to the coffee shop across the street. I grabbed a seat near the window and ordered breakfast. Pancakes and hot chocolate. My brain runs well on sugar.

While I waited for my food, I thought about how I'd eaten so many meals alone in the cafeteria at Edgeview, an outcast among a whole school of outcasts, until Martin had become my friend. He'd probably never understand how much he'd done for me. I hoped I could do something for him some day.

I stared out the window. Still no activity at the house. I

knew I'd gotten there too late to see them come in. But I figured they might go out at lunchtime. I ordered a bowl of
chili so I'd have an excuse to stay in the coffee shop, then lingered over it while I read my book. The lunchtime crowd
started to filter in. I ordered a burger.

Around twelve-thirty, the waitress gave me one of those
order-something-or-get-moving looks. I knew that if I ordered
more food, I'd end up so bloated I wouldn't be able to walk. I
guess I knew two other things. With me on the run, there
was probably no reason for those lab guys to be there. So, as-
suming Bowdler was out looking for me, the building was
empty. The other thing I knew was that I didn't want to go
back inside the place where I'd been kept prisoner and
treated like a lab rat.

But I had to go. Fear, bad memories, whatever complex
mess of emotions was holding me back, it didn't matter. I
had to go. It was like going to the doctor for a shot. You fear
it. You go. You do it. It's done.

*elsewhere . . .

THURSDAY MORNING, FEELING so hungry that the hunger didn't even seem real anymore, Martin only had to walk for two hours before he reached the outskirts of Sayerton. After another hour of wandering, he found the right street.

A yellow bus rolled past, filled with singing kids. "You guys don't know how lucky you are," Martin muttered as he headed up the street. When he reached the house, he paused on the porch. *Is this too weird?* How would Trash's parents feel about him showing up? Would it bring back painful memories?

He pressed the bell. Nobody answered. Martin waited, rang the bell again, waited some more, then sighed and walked back to the sidewalk. He figured he had two choices— go see Cheater, or crawl back home.

"Cheater," he said out loud. That was the better choice. Martin figured he'd traveled close to twenty miles already. So Cheater probably only lived ten or fifteen miles away. Even if he didn't catch a ride, he could make it in three or four hours. Or five. Or ten. Because walking was what he did. That was his new life. He walked. And he thirsted. And he hungered. And he walked some more. Life on the road definitely stunk.

"Hold on there."

Martin spun around as someone tapped him on the shoulder. It was a guy in a dark blue suit wearing sunglasses and an unreadable expression. His blue necktie was speckled with yellow dots. Across the street, the driver's door of a parked car hung open. "Are you a friend of the family?" the guy asked.

Martin skittered away a step. The guy's greatest shame was that he had failed the written exam for a promotion to division chief three times. Eventually, he'd quit to go into business for himself. Martin didn't care about that, and he certainly wasn't going to use the knowledge to spit out an insult, because the guy's greatest pride spooked him. The guy was proud that he'd carried out seventeen successful assassinations in his career, along with countless kidnappings, acts of sabotage, and a whole slew of violent activities. He was proud that he'd do anything for the right price, and do it well. Recently, he even helped fake the death of a teenage boy.

"You're kind of skittish," the guy said.

"I've been having a rough day," Martin said. He couldn't help staring at the guy's tie. Close up, the yellow dots on it turned out to be tiny smiley faces.

"So, like I said, are you a friend of the family?"

Am I a friend of the family?

A dozen lies shot through Martin's head. He figured he could pretend he'd gone to the wrong house. But if the guy spotted the lie, Martin knew he'd end up in trouble. Or at the bottom of a river with his neck snapped, his arms broken, and fifty pounds of iron chain wrapped around his body. The truth seemed harmless.

He nodded. "Sort of. I don't know the parents, but I went to school with their son, Eddie. He's dead."

"So why are you here?"

So you can kill me and still not get promoted.

"I ran away from home." As he heard his own words, Martin was hit by the reality of his situation for the first time.

The guy stared at him for a moment, then reached inside his jacket. Martin tensed, wondering whether there was any chance he could get away. He relaxed when he saw the guy wasn't pulling out a gun or a knife.

"You look hungry." The guy took a twenty out of his wallet. "I ran off when I was thirteen. Probably a mistake, but I survived."

Martin took the money. "Thanks." It was strange feeling grateful to someone who had killed seventeen people. He turned to walk off.

"Kid," the guy called.

"Yeah?"

"Be careful. There are a lot of dangerous folks out there."

Yeah, there sure are, Martin thought. *I hope I don't meet any more of them for a while.*

*desperate steps

AS I WAS paying my check at the coffee house, I reached out with my mind and pressed the doorbell at the lab. Nobody answered the ring. I stood on the sidewalk for several more minutes, trying to think of a good reason not to go back into that place. Fear was the best reason I came up with, but I knew it wasn't good enough.

Finally, I crossed the street, walked up the steps, and opened the lock. At first, the doorknob wouldn't turn. I realized my palm was sweaty. I wiped my hand on my pants, then opened the door.

It was definitely creepy going back inside. I closed the door behind me, then listened carefully for any sounds. Except for the ticking of a clock from the room to my left, and faint traffic noises from outside, there was nothing.

I went downstairs first. I didn't visit the room where I'd been kept. I had no desire to see that again. But I went into the supply room at the back of the hall and found the cabinet with the drugs. There were jars filled with all sorts of pills and small vials of various colored liquids.

I noticed three bottles of clear liquid on the top shelf. One was open and half empty. I removed the lid, touched the tip of my finger to the liquid, then touched my finger to my tongue. There was no taste, which by itself didn't tell me anything. But I opened one of the sealed bottles and carefully tasted that, again with my finger tip. This time, I instinctively spat out as the familiar, bitter flavor spread across my tongue. The two liquids were definitely different, though the labels were the same, with some long chemical name I couldn't even guess how to pronounce. If this was the stuff Bowdler had been giving me, someone had replaced my medicine with water. I had no idea why.

I headed for the office on the first floor. The file cabinets were locked. No problem. I unlocked them with my mind, slid open the top drawer, and scanned the tabs on the hanging folders. It was mostly electronics catalogues, old magazine articles, and other useless stuff.

Near the back was a fat folder with my name on it. I pulled it out and put it on the desk. Then I looked through the rest of the drawers, making sure there weren't files with my friends' names on them. I didn't see any, which I took as a good sign. Maybe Bowdler didn't know about the guys. Not yet. But if he dug into my past, there was a risk he'd figure out I wasn't the only one with a hidden talent.

I still had no idea who'd kidnapped me. There weren't any memos or letters or anything like that. The next room looked like some kind of electronics lab. There were a couple empty take-out cartons and a coffee cup on the work table, along with a jumble of scattered parts. Small pieces of wire littered the floor. All the other rooms I'd seen were neat and clean. I had the feeling someone had been working here all night assembling something.

I found a cardboard box that contained several small devices with lots of buttons on them. Each of the devices had a label attached with a rubber band. I read a couple of them, hoping I could find something useful, but they didn't mean anything to me. A handwritten note on top read: *Douglas, here are the prototypes of our current projects. I thought you might enjoy an advance look. Maybe you can work them into our next round of contracts. Feel free to be inventive.* It was signed with scrawled initials I couldn't make out.

None of the other rooms had anything interesting. I sat down to read my file. The stack of handwritten sheets didn't tell me much. It was mostly filled with the results of experiments. It looked like Bowdler had run hundreds of different tests. He'd drugged me pretty heavily at first, then adjusted the dosage until I was in a state where I'd do what he asked but not try to escape.

There were a bunch of references to people I'd never heard of. Stuff like: *subject shows much greater range than that attributed to Kalnikov* or *unlike accounts of Sherenova, subject is not hyper-susceptible to distractions.*

The last entry read, *The disrupter functions perfectly. We can proceed immediately with the miniaturized version.*

Disrupter? I wondered what that was. I skimmed some of the earlier pages, but none of the other entries mentioned it. There was also nothing about my family, or about any plans for me after the experiments were done. Maybe he was just going to lock me away forever, or burn me up for real. I fought down the urge to destroy the place. It was better if I left no trace of my visit. I didn't want him to know I was still in town.

I'd learned all I could here. I put the file back where I'd found it and checked around to make sure I hadn't disturbed anything. But there was one more thing I could do before I left. I figured a lot of stuff never got printed out, and wouldn't be in the file cabinets. The important stuff could all be on the computer. My MP3 player also worked as a flash drive. I went to one of the computers, plugged into the USB port, and copied the documents folder.

That's when I heard a key in the door. I yanked out the MP3 player and looked around for a place to hide.

"You're good with locks, my young friend," someone called from the hallway. "But you know nothing about alarms. That's why you need me. I can teach you."

Bowdler's voice was like a shot of sulfuric acid pumped directly into my veins. I hadn't even thought there'd be an alarm. My desire to hurt him went to war with my desire not to look into those eyes again. The last time I'd lashed out in panic, I'd killed someone. If I did that now, I'd never get answers to my questions. I needed a minute to calm myself and figure out how to do this right.

I ducked behind the desk. There was a window in the wall facing the street. Staying hidden, I raised the window as quickly and as noisily as I could.

From where I crouched, I heard Bowdler run down the hall. I could see him through a gap beneath the top of the desk. He strolled into the room and headed for the window.

He had a gun in one hand and a small, unpainted metal box in the other.

I couldn't tell whether the gun was the kind that fired darts or real bullets. Either way, I didn't want to get shot. If he knocked me out now, I'd never see the streets of Philadelphia again.

As he leaned out the window, I reached out with my mind to yank the gun from his hand. Once he was disarmed, I could make him tell me everything I needed to know.

Nothing happened.

I tried again. Nothing.

I felt like someone had just cut off my arms. I tried harder. I tried with all the strength my mind could generate, but it was useless. The gun might as well have been made of air. My power didn't touch it. Why? Was it that thing he carried? Was that what a disrupter did? I remember when I'd failed to move the marble in the lab. He must have been testing the disrupter. I stayed still and waited for him to climb through the window.

"Nice try, Eddie," he said. "You're pretty clever for an amateur." He stepped away from the window and scanned the room. "But you're no match for professionals."

Think!

I was so used to depending on my talent, it was hard to imagine any other solution.

"Eddie, I'm not in the mood for hide and seek. We have a lot of work to do. There's nothing to worry about. No more nasty medicine, I promise. We don't need that anymore."

I held my breath as Bowdler's eyes locked on the desk,

then nearly jumped as a harsh squawk burst through the air. He put the box on the window ledge and pulled a walkie-talkie from a clip on his belt.

"Any sign of him outside?" He paused a moment, then said, "I didn't think so. He's still in here." He shook his head. "No. Maintain your position. I want you out front if he makes a break for the door. Don't worry about the back. He can't clear the wall."

So there was at least one other person outside, and Bowdler was about to start searching for me. I had a feeling he was very good at hide and seek. Or search and destroy. I couldn't just wait here and hope he didn't find me.

But there was no way I was going to jump him. He had a gun, he was way bigger than I was, and he probably knew all sorts of deadly fighting techniques. The only thing I had going for me was surprise.

I waited until he looked down to clip the walkie-talkie back onto his belt. There was a heavy tape dispenser on the desk. I grabbed it, stood up, and threw it as hard as I could. But not at him. Hoping I was right, I aimed for the box on the window sill. If that's what was blocking my power, I had a chance to get out of here. Even as the dispenser left my hand, I found myself trying to guide it with my mind. But that wasn't necessary. I hit the box with a solid shot, sending it flying out the window. I heard it clatter to the street. Broken, I hoped. If not, I was definitely in deep trouble.

Bowdler spun toward me. I reached out with my mind and ripped the gun from his hand. It flew up with so much force, it smashed through the plasterboard of the ceiling. He was lucky it didn't take his trigger finger with it.

I had my power back. I could do anything I wanted to him. I could snap his ribs or rip his heart out through his mouth. I could pluck his eyesballs from their sockets and force him to juggle them.

The gun must have cut him when I yanked it away. Blood spilled from a gash in his palm. I hesitated for an instant, fighting the memories brought on by the sight. I had to stop him, but I didn't want to live with the burden of another death.

Unlike me, Bowdler didn't hesitate. He dived backward and rolled out the window. "Give me your disrupter," he shouted.

I raced into the hallway. I knew I couldn't go out the front. I ran to the rear of the house. By the time I reached the door, I'd unlocked it and flung it open with my mind. I leaped out the back, my feet barely even touching the porch steps, and ran as fast as I could. There was a brick wall behind the house at least ten feet high. Maybe more. It was higher than I could jump. I couldn't lift myself more than a couple inches. The times I'd tried anything like that, I'd ended up sprawled on my butt.

I heard footsteps racing down the hallway. I searched the yard for something I could use as a ladder. No tables. No chairs. Not even a large flower pot. But there were some left-over bricks scattered on the ground.

I stacked three bricks, end to end, two feet away from the

wall. Keeping those in place, I stacked six more bricks a foot from the wall to the left of the first stack. As I ran toward my emergency stairs, I pressed nine bricks against the wall, in line with the first three, and hoped I could hold everything in place under my weight.

I reached the first stack, stepped on it with my right foot, landed on the second stack with my left, then hit the third with my right. I felt like I'd just been plunged into a real-life video game. As I leaped to the top of the wall, I let the bricks topple back down behind me.

The other side of the wall led to more backyards. I jumped down, then cut around a house and onto the street, sprinting full out, like Death himself was on my tail. I ran until I couldn't even breathe, and then ran some more. Finally, I stopped and risked a glance over my shoulder. There was no sign of Bowdler. But I knew I couldn't stay in the city. They'd be searching for me, swarming through the city like wasps from a busted nest. I had no idea how many people Bowdler had at his disposal. I needed to get out of Philadelphia. But first, I had to become someone else.

*elsewhere . . .

AS MARTIN HEADED down the street, he wondered what Trash's parents had done to bring this sort of trouble to their doorstep. And he wondered whether he should try to warn them. He had no way to get in touch with them. But there was still something he could do.

When he reached town, he called 911 from a pay phone and told the dispatcher, "There's a car parked across the street from eight-thirty-four Harbor Road. There's a guy in it. He has a gun."

He wasn't sure that was true, though it was hard to imagine that the guy wasn't armed. He probably had a gun, a knife or two, and maybe a small atom bomb. At least the police would come and check him out.

Having done all he could, Martin headed for a corner diner to put some food in his grumbling stomach. He sat at the counter and wolfed down a grilled cheese sandwich. He was dying to eat more, but he wanted to save as much of the cash as possible. The waitress told him where he could catch a bus that would take him a good part of the way toward Cheater's house. She was so nice, he felt bad about leaving her a crummy tip. But he knew she was proud of her daughter, so he asked her if she had any kids and listened politely while she bragged.

Once he got off the bus, he only had to walk two more miles. This time, someone was home. A kid who looked like an older, bigger, version of Cheater answered the door. He was eating an apple.

"Is Dennis here?" Martin asked.

The guy shook his head, chewed for a moment, then said, "Nope. The stupid jerk got himself beat up."

"What?"

The guy shrugged and wiped a dribble of juice from his chin. "My dipwad little brother managed to get the snot stomped out of himself in some fleabag motel. Not very smart. Our parents are on a trip, so guess who had to deal with it? I'm always getting stuck." He started to close the door.

Martin put his hand on the door. "Where is he?"

"Philly. That hospital where they treat kids with thick heads."

"I'm a friend of his. Martin Anderson. He ever mention me?" Martin hoped Cheater's brother would at least invite him in. Or maybe offer him a ride to Philly.

The guy shook his head, then wrinkled up his nose. "Man, you really smell. Ever heard of soap?" He shut the door.

"I guess I'm going to Philly," Martin said.

*radical disguise

I FLED TOWARD the train station, scanning the stores I passed in search of a new identity. I finally found a place that sold extreme hair color in a can. I'd learned something from the pajamas—you can try to avoid stares, or you can force people to look away. I couldn't think of any easy way to avoid getting recognized, so I figured I'd try to make myself so radical that anyone looking for Eddie Thalmayer wouldn't give me a second glance.

Red, green, black, or white? My hair was light brown. I went for black. I grabbed three fake nose rings, some hair gel, a spiked wrist band, and a Ramones t-shirt—probably more stuff than I needed, but I didn't want to waste time thinking it over. I paid, headed for the door, then froze. Carrying the stuff wouldn't do me any good.

"You have a bathroom?" I asked the girl at the counter.

She shook her head. "It's not for public use."

I gave her my best lost-puppy look. I also gave her lungs the tiniest squeeze, so she'd feel her heart flutter and her breath speed up. It was a cheap trick, but I didn't have much choice.

Her expression softened. "Oh, why not. It's in the back."

"Thanks." I went into the bathroom and transformed myself into every parent's nightmare. To make the change complete, I hunched over, like the whole world was pulling me down with more force than I could bear. It was a posture I was familiar with.

"Thanks again," I said to the girl when I came back out.

She didn't blink at the change. In fact, she smiled. "Hey," she called after me as I went out the door, "you doing anything tonight?"

"Yeah, sorry. I expect to be tied up later."

As soon as I hit the street, I knew I'd picked the right costume. People would stare for an instant as I walked toward them, then look away, as if the image stung their eyes. They noticed me, but they didn't really see me. I was radically shielded.

But I'd feel a whole lot better once I got out of Philadelphia and headed for some other city. Preferably a big one. Maybe I'd go to New York. It would be easy enough to disappear once I got there. I'd figure it out when I reached the station.

Every time I saw someone in a dark suit heading toward me, my breath sped up. I knew the whole world wasn't searching for me. That would be a crazy thought. But somebody was trying to find me.

I reached the alley where I'd stashed my backpack, floated it down, then crossed over to the train station. I spotted a guy in a blue suit right by the main entrance. He was just standing there holding a tiny yellow shopping bag. Guys in suits don't carry shopping bags. Not unless they're with a lady who's shopping. None of the men I'd seen earlier had a bag. Maybe it had taken Bowdler a while to get more of those disrupters made. If this guy had one of them in the bag, I'd be powerless. I tried to move a candy wrapper that was crumpled on the ground near his feet. It didn't budge.

I wanted to turn and run. I was sure he'd grab me when I went past. My disguise stunk. What was I thinking? He'd knock me out and take me back to Bowdler.

The guy glanced at the small photo in his other hand, then scanned the crowd. I froze as his eyes moved past me. He stared at me for an instant, then shook his head in disgust and looked away.

He didn't recognize me. Still expecting to be grabbed, I walked past him, then slipped over to a corner of the terminal and studied the departure information on the big board that hung over the information desk. Maybe New York was a bad idea. They'd probably expect me to go somewhere like that. For all I knew, they had guys in Penn Station, watching everyone who arrived from Philly.

It would be better if I went to New Jersey first, and then to New York. There was a train leaving for Trenton in five minutes. That would work.

I bought a ticket and headed across the terminal toward the stairs that led to the platform for my train. I saw another guy in a suit ahead of me. I looked down, trying to make myself invisible. A crowd was coming in my direction. I guess another train had just arrived. Good. The more people around me, the better. Crowds were my friend.

I kept my attention glued to the floor. Once I got past this last guy, I could go down the steps and get on the train. Despite the crowd, I wasn't bumped much. Even without checking around me, I could tell that people were avoiding contact with someone who looked as creepy as I did. I almost enjoyed the feeling that nobody wanted anything to do with me.

*elsewhere . . .

MARTIN WAITED WHILE the rest of the passengers rushed off the train. He hated getting jostled in crowds. The flood of impressions he received was a heavy load to carry. Every person he bumped into left him with the details of his or her greatest prides and deepest sorrows.

Finally, he left the train. There was hardly anyone on the stairs, but the crowd grew denser when he got up to the terminal.

Luckily, he saw a break ahead. There was a punky-looking kid coming toward him. People were moving wide of the kid, as if the air around him was poisoned. That was good. It gave Martin more room to slip through without getting jostled as much.

Even so, he couldn't completely shelter himself. At least he was used to it after a year weaving through the crowded halls at his high school. Impressions flittered through his mind with each jostle. *I'm so good at trading stocks. I hate my body. I wish I'd learned to play the guitar. I can move things with my mind. I have a photographic memory. I beat my dog. I make the best blueberry pies in the world.*

Martin spun around as one impression seized him. *I can move things with my mind.*

Trash! But Trash was dead. Martin searched through his memory for anything paired with the pride. *I can move things with my mind. I draw awesome spaceships. My parents don't spend much time with me.*

He scanned the crowd of people who'd just passed him. There were only three kids in the group—a little girl, a guy in his midteens, and the spiked-hair kid in a ripped Ramones shirt.

Martin didn't recognize the punk kid. But the walk—the way he moved, slunk down like the world was pressing on him—that was familiar. Amazingly familiar. He remembered the way Trash had acted at Edgeview before he'd learned about his talent. He'd been beaten down by everything. Almost crushed out of existence.

It couldn't be him. Trash was dead. It said so in the paper. But that guy at Trash's house—he'd faked a kid's death. Martin sped toward the kid, trying to reach him before he boarded a train. The closer he got, the surer he was. If he was right, this would erase all the sorrow he'd carried with him since that terrible day. *I have to be right,* Martin thought. He didn't know if he could handle the pain of being wrong.

the power of two

AS I HEADED for the stairs, I sensed someone behind me. The footsteps matched my own. I sped up. So did the steps that followed me. I wanted to run. But that would be a mistake. Running would get me noticed. Notice would get me caught.

Someone whispered in my ear. Three words. "Be cool, Trash."

I glanced back and gasped at the sight of the brown-haired, blue-eyed guy in the plain green t-shirt. Suddenly, everything seemed so much better. I slowed my pace and let Martin catch up with me. "Man, am I glad to see you."

"Tell me about it," Martin said. "You're supposed to be dead." He'd grown a bit since last year. But so had I, which meant I was still a head taller and twenty pounds heavier.

I kept my voice quiet and my eyes straight ahead. "It's a long story. Most of which I don't know. But we have to get out of here. There are people looking for me."

"Yeah. Serious guys in blue suits," Martin said. "Like the one we just passed. That's why I didn't shout. There's one outside your house, too. They aren't playing around."

"I know. So I can't go home. But I have to go somewhere. I was figuring maybe Trenton, and then New York."

"We can't leave. Cheater's here, in the hospital. He's been hurt."

"How bad?" I wondered if Bowdler was involved.

"I don't know. But I'm headed there to find out."

I looked at the train car that was just a couple steps away. Philadelphia was swarming with people who were searching for me. They had disrupters, guns, and probably all sorts of high-tech stuff I didn't even know existed. Trenton would be safe. But Cheater was one of my few real friends. He'd never run out on me if I was hurt. "Let's go."

I turned and headed up the stairs and out of the station, back past the men in suits with their shopping bags. I waited until we were across the street from the station before speaking again. "You don't know anything else about Cheater?"

"His brother said he got beaten up. And his parents are on a trip. That's all I know." Martin stared at me as we walked. "So, when did you decide to make a fashion statement?"

"About half an hour ago. You like it?"

"Not really. I think you should shave it all off and start over."

As we walked to the hospital, I filled him in on everything that had happened, keeping my voice low, afraid that any of the hundreds of people we passed might latch onto my words, see through my disguise, and shoot me with a dart before I could react. I skipped over the worst part until I'd told him the rest. Finally, I described the moment when I'd killed that man.

Martin stopped walking and turned to me. "You can't change the past."

"I know. But that doesn't help. I can't get the image out of my mind. Or the guilt."

"From what you told me about Bowdler, the real problem might be that you killed the wrong guy."

"Maybe."

Martin shook his head. "Man, I thought I had a tough time adjusting. I mean, I survived some rough stuff at school this year. Walking through the halls and absorbing all that heavy angst from everyone was like reading fifty teen problem novels at once. But you've got me beat."

"This is one contest I'd be happy to lose," I said. "Makes me wonder what's happening to the rest of the guys. If this disrupter works on all of us, we're pretty much at Bowdler's mercy."

"Torchie's fine," Martin said. "I get letters from him all the time. I think he's the last kid on the planet who uses snail mail. I can tell how he's doing by how scorched the paper is. And I got an e-mail from Flinch last week. He sent me some jokes he's working on. I haven't heard anything from Lucky in a while, and he hasn't answered any of my e-mails. I think Cheater's been trying to get in touch with him. And you're dead. Not to mention pretty funny looking."

I punched him on the shoulder. "I missed you."

"Me, too."

It was good to hear that Torchie and Flinch were okay. I guess Bowdler didn't know about anyone else. But I was worried that the guys hadn't heard from Lucky. Though, right now, I was more worried about Cheater.

When we reached the hospital, I paused by the front entrance.

"What's wrong?" Martin asked.

"You sure you want to be with me? This isn't some game, like sneaking out of Edgeview or taking on a couple bullies. The bad guys have guns. They seem to make up their own laws, too."

"I'm sure," Martin said. "You know me—the bigger they act, the more stubborn I get. At least, that's what nine out of ten psychologists say. Come on, we've got a friend to see."

A PHONE CONVERSATION BETWEEN MAJOR BOWDLER AND AN UNNAMED TECHNICIAN AT A COUNTER-INTELLIGENCE FACILITY IN FORT MEADE, MARYLAND

BOWDLER: This is Bowdler.

TECHNICIAN: Yes. Go ahead.

BOWDLER: I need a filter for the following name . . .

TECHNICIAN: Ready.

BOWDLER: Eddie Thalmayer. All variations—Ed, Edward.

TECHNICIAN: National?

BOWDLER: East Coast for now. Priority ten. Land lines and cellular.

TECHNICIAN: It's in place.

BOWDLER: I'm also uploading frontal and profile facial images for real-time recognition.

TECHNICIAN: Noted. We'll alert you to any hits. Be advised the system is currently running at a backlog.

while trash and martin are heading for the hospital, lucky stands on his own two feet . . .

"**IT'S TIME FOR** a walk."

Lucky stared at the smiling nurse, wishing she'd go away. She smelled like rubbing alcohol and mouthwash. Back in the other place, one of the nurses dragged him out of his room and made him do stuff once or twice a day. Sometimes it was a jigsaw puzzle, sometimes it was stupid crafts. Mostly, it was walks. This place was no different. He felt like someone's German shepherd. Besides, he'd just gotten here this morning, and wasn't even used to his new room.

"Come on, Dominic," the nurse said. "Exercise is important. You'll feel better. Trust me."

No way. He didn't trust anyone. And he didn't want to get out of bed. But he knew she'd nag him until he did what she asked. He stood up and followed her down the corridor and out through the locked doors that separated his ward from the rest of the hospital. His slippers scuffed against the floor with each step. Her cushioned heels tapped the floor with the rhythm of a pendulum.

At least there weren't any lost objects in the hallways crying out for his attention. Hospitals were constantly swept clean of everything—dirt, germs, hopes. Though the voices wouldn't have been much of a problem. The medicine kept them from bothering him.

"You're so lucky," the nurse whispered as they turned a corner into the main corridor. "Some of these poor children are very sick. It's so sad."

Yeah, I'm lucky, he thought. There was no way to explain to her that his own problems were just as bad. Maybe his heart was fine and his kidneys weren't failing. Maybe his bones weren't broken and his flesh wasn't burned. But there were other ways to suffer. The stuff nobody else could see—that was probably the worst kind of suffering to bear. Even if he told them, they wouldn't understand. But he couldn't tell them. If they knew about his hidden talent, they'd do terrible things to him.

He stopped dead as he glanced into one of the rooms. A quiz show was playing on a TV in the far corner. There was a kid in the first bed who looked familiar. The kid kept shouting out answers, even though nobody was in the room. After each answer, he'd moan and grab his face, which was all bruised and puffed up. Lucky was sure he knew him.

He thought about calling out, but the nurse gave him a gentle tap on the shoulder. "Give him his privacy. He's had a rough time. Let's go, Dominic."

Lucky moved on. He knew he could remember who the kid was if he tried hard enough, but he was happy to stop thinking and just drift back into the haze. The real world was far too harsh to visit for any length of time.

*haunting the hallways

WE STOPPED AT the information desk and found out what room Cheater was in, then took the elevator to the fourth floor.

"You'd better let me go in first," Martin said.

"Why?"

"You want him to think he's seeing ghosts, dead boy?"

"Good point."

I followed Martin down the hall to Cheater's room, but waited out of sight while he went inside. A moment later, I heard Cheater shout, "He's alive!" I couldn't help smiling. It sounded like a line from one of those old horror movies he loved.

That shout was immediately followed by a howl of pain, which also could have come from a horror movie. I guess Cheater's face was sore. I stepped into the room. One bed was empty. The other had a kid who resembled a badly sculpted version of my friend.

"You look good for a ghost," he said through puffed lips.

"You look awful for a living person." I could see why it would hurt him to shout. He was so bruised, he could have passed for the twin brother of an eggplant. "Though you don't look bad for a corpse."

Cheater nodded. "Exquisite corpse."

"What?" Martin asked.

That was one piece of trivia I knew, since it involved some of my favorite artists. But I didn't want to spoil Cheater's fun, so I let him explain.

"Exquisite corpse is the name of a word game the surrealist painters played," he said. "They'd write a phrase on a piece of paper and then—" He stopped and scrunched up his face in pain.

"Hurts to talk?" I asked.

He nodded again.

"Maybe you should let us do the talking."

"Like Cyrano de Bergerac?" he asked.

He had me with that one. I was clueless. But I didn't wait for an explanation. "So, you're okay?" I asked.

"Yeah. I have a new understanding of some of the finer aspects of physics. Astronomy, too. I saw a lot more than stars. Constellations, at the very least. I think I might have also witnessed the big bang. Ouch." He grabbed his face and groaned.

"You keep talking, I'm going to have to smack you," Martin said.

Cheater grinned at him, which also seemed to hurt. "I miss the way you always kidded me. It reminds me—"

"I'm not kidding," Martin said. "Give your face a rest. Trash has a lot to tell you."

I described how I'd been abducted, and Martin told him

about running away. Cheater tried to keep his mouth shut, but he couldn't help interrupting us every minute or two to toss in some essential facts.

"Now what?" he asked when we were done.

"Not sure," I said. "Hide out, think up a plan."

"It better be a good plan. This disrupter is really bad news," he said. "Are you going to stick around Philly?"

"Not sure about that, either," I said. I was tired of hunching down and waiting for someone to shove me in a van or shoot me in the neck with another dart.

"I think we have to stay around," Martin said. "That's the only way we can find out what's going on. The answer isn't in Trenton. Or in New York. It's here. Even if they can block your power, or maybe even all of our powers, this is where we need to be. This Bowdler guy sounds like someone who won't give up until he gets what he wants. You can't run from that."

"Besides," Cheater said, "I think Lucky is down the hall. And I'm pretty sure he's in worse shape than I am."

"You saw him here?" I asked.

"Just a little while ago," Cheater said. "I just caught a glimpse, but the nurse called him 'Dominic,' and it sure looked like him."

"Let's check it out."

Martin and I went down the hall and tried to find out about Lucky. The nurse at the desk wouldn't tell us anything.

I was about to give up when Martin said to her, "You look familiar."

He stared at her for a moment, then said, "Were you in *Guys and Dolls* last month?"

She beamed a huge smile at him. "Yes. At the community playhouse. You saw it?"

"You were marvelous. I went with my friend Dominic Calabrizi. He loves musicals even more than I do. You should sing a song for him when you have the chance."

"I will. The poor boy. He's been through so much." She gulped, glanced around, and added, "I shouldn't talk about the patients."

"Of course."

Martin turned away.

"That was amazing," I said once we'd moved away from the desk.

"It's no big deal."

We went back to Cheater's room. "Lucky's definitely here."

"I'll see if I can learn anything," Cheater said.

We talked a bit more, but I could tell Cheater was pretty tired. I figured he'd get more rest if we left. On my way out of the room, I paused and looked back. "Are you sure you're okay?"

"I'm a quick healer. The human body is amazingly re-silient. There was a book about a guy, Phineas Gauge, who survived getting a spike through his head. And I heard about this woman whose parachute didn't open, but she survived her fall. There are even cases of spontaneous healing. Little kids can sometimes grow back a severed finger."

"I'll take that as a yes," I said. He might have gotten stomped, but it hadn't crushed his enthusiasm for weird facts.

"At least we can rule out brain damage," Martin said after we'd left the hospital.

"Yeah, he'll be fine." I sniffed the air as we walked down the street. "But you're getting kind of ripe."

"I've been on the road a bit."

"Crawling through Dumpsters?"

"Nothing that luxurious."

"Got any other clothes?"

He shook his head. "Just what I'm wearing."

"We may have to burn them. With you in them. I'd share my stuff, but there's no way any of it would fit you. Looks like we have some shopping to do."

After we'd bought clothes for Martin, I said, "Let's get a room. We need to figure out what to do. And you need a shower."

"How are we going to get a room? Nobody's going to let a couple kids check into a hotel. Especially not Stinky and Spikey."

"Sure they will," I said. "And I think you're going to like the place."

FROM FLINCH'S JOKE JOURNAL

I'm writing this in a limo. A long, white sucker, with a TV in it. How slick is that? We're going to this fancy hotel, and we get to stay all weekend. There's gotta be some good stuff about this I can use in my act.

"The limo was so long, when I called the driver it was a long-distance call."

Not bad. Sounds awkward. Needs to be smoother. But it's a keeper. What else? I need something I can use tonight.

"They brought me here in a limo. But I'm confused about one thing. Is the passenger supposed to pay for the gas?"

Nah. That one stinks. Maybe something about how if I'm funny enough I won't have to pay for the gas next time. What else is going on? Devon's here as my chaperone, but as soon as we check in, he's going to split and go see his friends at Drexel.

"My cousin Devon likes to party. We call him 'blackjack' because ever since he turned 21, he's been trying hard to make sure he never hits 22."

Good one. That's a keeper. I am so pumped for tonight. This is one trip I'll never forget.

checking in

"NO WAY THEY'RE going to let us in here." Martin pointed toward the hotel entrance, where a half-dozen doormen greeted people driving luxury cars.

"Sure they will," I said. I watched a long, white limo leave the hotel and pull into the street. Two cabs tried to shoot into the opening.

"Looking like this?" Martin asked.

He had a point. Money talked. But some things could still drown it out. "Hang on." I pulled out the fake rings and took off the wrist band. Then I slicked down my hair as much as I could. There wasn't anything I could do about the color. I was glad I'd gone with black.

"Presentable?" I asked Martin.

He nodded, then pointed past me. "Hey, that guy looks like Flinch."

I watched the guy who was walking out of the hotel. "Yeah. Sort of. But older."

We headed into the lobby. "Play along," I said. "Feel free to use your talent. Just stand far enough behind me so the clerk can't smell you."

Martin stared around at the lobby. "I'm feeling a little out of place."

"That's their plan. Hotels like this want to intimidate unwelcome visitors. Our plan is to ignore that." I walked right up to the front desk, trying very hard to pretend I was someone like my dad, who was comfortable anywhere. He'd told me more than once that money, by itself, didn't earn respect.

I was hoping the clerk didn't feel that way. He eyed me from top to bottom, looking for clues to whether I would be a good or bad part of his day. I could be anyone—a lost kid, a guest who had already checked in, a scammer coming in off the street, or, as far as I wanted him to believe, the son of a very rich and slightly odd woman.

"Can I help you?" he asked.

I nodded, trying to give out the proper mix of annoyance and embarrassment. "Mother decided to go shopping. Like she doesn't already have enough stuff. At least she dropped us off first. We're so sick of watching her buy shoes. But she forgot to make a reservation." I shook my head and muttered, "Typical."

"Did she give you her—"

I cut him off. "Mother doesn't believe in credit cards." I looked him right in the eye so we could exchange annoyed glances and let each other know how inconvenient this was. "Mother believes in cash. She adores Mr. Franklin and Mr. Jefferson." I pulled a fistful of bills out of my pocket. "She asked me to check us in."

He stared at the cash. I could see him thinking it over. The whole world revolved around plastic. Cash was unusual.

"Sorry," I said. "I know it's a pain. You should see when she buys a car. She makes us lug in bags of cash. It's thoroughly ridiculous. I thought I'd pull a muscle when she bought that Maserati. You know what one of those things costs?"

The man nodded, but I could see he still wasn't completely buying the act. I looked over at Martin, hoping he'd say something to make the guy like us, but he seemed to have turned to stone. Then I glanced past him to the left wall, where a copy of an old painting hung in a heavy wooden frame.

"Caravaggio," I said, identifying the artist. "Very nice."

Art is one of the common languages of people who stay at overpriced hotels. They know Dürer, Klee, and dozens of other passwords. I'd just showed the guy I was a member of the right group. I could have told him the title of the painting, but I didn't want to overdo it.

He smiled and slid a form across the counter for me to fill out. "One night?"

"Let's make it two, for now. Of course, Mother might decide to stay longer." I made up a name and address, slid back the form, and paid for the room. I added a tip, since that was also part of our common language.

A minute later, I had my key card. Five minutes after that, Martin and I were standing inside a very comfortable room, fifteen stories above the streets of Philadelphia.

"Sorry I didn't help," he said.

"You helped. I don't think I'd have had the guts to do that if I was by myself." I pointed toward the shower. "Feel free to use all the soap. They'll make more."

I ordered some food from room service while Martin washed up. I felt bad for him. He'd had a lousy time on the road. I'd bet he could have used his talent to make things more comfortable. He could have talked people into giving him stuff, because he knew what they were proud about. I think most people, if you stroke their egos, can't help liking you.

My dad was a master at that. He didn't have any special power—he just knew how to make people like him. But Martin never had as much faith in his own talent as he had in everyone else's. And he had this problem with using his power for his advantage. I didn't see anything wrong with it. If I could add numbers faster than anyone else, I'd make use of that talent. If I could jump higher than anyone else, I'd jump whenever I could. If I can move things with my mind, why not use my talent?

"So what's the plan?" Martin asked when he came out of the bathroom. He'd gotten dressed in his new clothes, but was still toweling his hair dry. Then he caught sight of the meal I'd had delivered. "You talk. I'll eat."

"I don't have a clue," I said as I watched him inhale a burger in three bites. "What I want to do is run away from here. I want to go so far that they'll never find me."

"That's no way to live," Martin said. "You'd be hiding from every stranger you see. It'd be like those guys in the witness protection program."

"I know. So I've got to deal with this, somehow."

Martin pointed to the remaining stack of food. "Right after I clean my plate."

We talked until late in the night, catching up on stuff and trying to think up a plan. We'd done so well before, at Edgeview. But there had been six of us, and we'd known exactly who our enemies were.

"This is hopeless," I said before we went to sleep.

"Hey," Martin said. "Yesterday, I slept in an alley on pieces of cardboard. I was starving and I stunk." He patted the plush comforter that he'd pulled down to the foot of his bed. "Look at me now. My bed is soft, my stomach is full . . ." He paused to sniff the back of his hand, then said, ". . . and I smell like lemons. So don't ever tell me anything or anyone is hopeless."

"Except you," I muttered. But the mutter masked a grin.

AFTER PART THREE
BUT
BEFORE PART FOUR
SO CALL IT
PART THREE POINT FIVE

wherein
various forms of
travel produce various results

friday morning peregrination #1

BOWDLER TAKES A RIDE AND FAILS TO KILL ANYONE

MAJOR BOWDLER KNEW he was wasting his time, but he needed to keep moving so the swelling rage wouldn't cloud his thoughts. He drove through Center City, scanning the pedestrians in hopes of finding the escapee.

He can't get away.

There was no way a fourteen-year-old civilian could remain hidden for long against all the resources Bowdler had at his disposal. The instant the boy used his established e-mail account, he'd be located. The moment he uttered his name on the phone, the massive computers buried beneath the counter-intelligence facility would recognize it and report his location. If he passed within range of any video surveillance equipment tied to the system, he would leave a trail.

It's just a matter of time.

Bowdler glanced ahead as the traffic light half a block away turned green. A young woman, her head bobbing to music pumped into her skull through earbuds, crossed against the light. Bowdler gauged her distance and pressed down slightly on the accelerator. His car skimmed past her, close enough so she could feel the breeze against her knees. Perfect. Maybe that would give her enough of a scare so she'd pay attention next time. He didn't bother to look in the mirror to see her reaction.

A block later, a dented red Chevy pickup truck ran a stop sign. Bowdler slammed his brakes, then leaned on the horn. The pickup cruised on like nothing had happened. "Idiot," Bowdler muttered as he glared at the back of the truck. The driver seemed to be reading a map.

He drove for an hour, sticking to Center City. As he neared Franklin Circle, he spotted another jaywalker. This one, a teen who looked the same age as the escapee, was crossing in the middle of the block, obviously not paying any attention to traffic. The boy slowed his pace. Bowdler changed lanes, swerving to the left so he could brush past his target as close as possible.

At the last instant, the boy skipped back, as if he'd been more aware of his surroundings than his posture indicated.

Good for you, young man. Feeling a bit better, Bowdler headed toward the containment facility where the subject would be taken as soon as he was recaptured. He needed to have a word with the other detainee, and decide whether it was time yet to cancel him.

friday morning peregrination #2

LUCKY TAKES A WALK AND HEARS A NEW VOICE
IN THE FOG

ANOTHER WALK. DIFFERENT nurse. A guy named Nick. Lucky shuffled along next to him, wondering how much time there was before his next pill.

"Lucky."

That wasn't supposed to happen. The medicine should muffle the voices.

"Lucky, come back."

He walked several steps past the open doorway before he understood why the voice was so clear. It was coming from a real person. He turned back.

"Where you going, sport?" Nick asked.

"Someone called me," Lucky said.

"I didn't hear nobody say Dominic."

"He called me 'Lucky.' That's my nickname."

Nick snorted out a laugh, then shook his head. "Sorry, dude. I guess it's not that funny."

"Lucky," the voice called again.

"Can I see who it is?" Lucky asked.

"I suppose it's okay to peek in and see if he's really calling you."

Lucky walked to the room. He didn't recognize the bruised, swollen face.

"Lucky," the kid said, "it's me. Cheater."

Next to him, he heard Nick say, "Lucky, Cheater. What next? Sleepy, Dopey, and Goofy?"

"It's not Goofy," the kid said. "It's Grumpy." He listed the seven dwarfs, then started to talk about the origin of Goofy as a character called "Dippy Dog."

Lucky took another step into the room. He knew that voice. He recognized the way an endless stream of information flowed from that mouth. His brain slowly made sense of the unexpected images. This was Cheater. His old friend. Without his glasses. All banged up, and moaning after every couple of words. "What happened?"

"I stayed when I should have folded."

"You okay?"

"I'll live. Guess what? I have great news."

"What?"

Cheater stared past him, toward Nick. "Nothing. Hey, what are you doing here?"

Lucky knew it wouldn't be good to talk too much. He and Cheater had dangerous secrets. He stumbled over to the bed and thought about all that had happened. He swished it around in his mind and tried to keep it there as long as possible, like a big mouthful of stinging mouthwash.

A moment later, Nick tapped Lucky on the shoulder. "Come on, Unlucky. We can't hang here too long."

Lucky followed Nick out of the room. When he looked back, he saw that Cheater was reaching for the phone on the small table next to his bed.

friday morning peregrination #3

TORCHIE TAKES A RIDE AND EVENTUALLY ARRIVES

"**WOW, I THINK** we've seen the whole city," Torchie said. He glanced to his left. Mr. Wickman was hunched over the wheel, looking all around, and then down at the map clutched in his right hand. Behind them, a horn blared. Philadelphia sure was a noisy place.

"It's got to be somewhere," Mr. Wickman said. "Everything is somewhere."

"We'll find it." They'd been driving around for an hour, searching for the hotel. Mr. Wickman didn't seem to be very good at following directions. And it was really distracting the way so many people were blowing their horns.

At last, Torchie spotted a small sign on a pole at the corner of a parking lot. "There," he said. "The Hillville Luxury Motel."

"I guess we found it." Mr. Wickman drove into the lot. The red pickup bounced as it crossed potholes of various depths.

Torchie saw several kids walking around with accordions. Nobody had an instrument anywhere near as large as his.

"You want me to come in with you?" Mr. Wickman asked.

"No. That's okay." Torchie slid out and grabbed his accordion. "Thanks for the ride."

"My pleasure." Mr. Wickman pulled back into the street.

Torchie flinched at the blaring of another car horn, then went inside.

friday morning peregrination #4

FLINCH TAKES A WALK AND FAILS TO DIE

"YOU'RE NOT FUNNY."

"You're not smelly. Wait—we're both wrong."

Lying in bed on Friday morning, half awake, Flinch grinned as he relived his favorite moments of last night. He always tried to be hard on himself and look for any flaws in his act, but he had to admit that he'd been on fire. Big time.

"Hey—you ain't ready for the big city."

"That's why I'm starting in Philly."

That one had been risky. He knew any performer took a chance when he knocked the town where he was playing. But he also knew that most cities liked to joke about themselves.

There'd been a couple spots that weren't as smooth as he'd like, but he was pretty happy with the way the night had gone. The limo had brought him to the club. He'd hung out all evening with the other comics backstage. They'd treated him okay. Now, awake and hungry, he had one thing on his mind.

"Breakfast," Flinch said. He knew he could get something at the hotel, but he had a craving that couldn't be denied.

He got dressed and headed out. It wasn't hard to follow his nose to the nearest place offering fresh, hot donuts.

Walking back to the hotel, his stomach and mind both full of warm memories, he crossed in the middle of the block. It was still early and traffic was light.

He saw the car in time. Ahead of time, actually. The idiot swerved across two empty lanes at the last moment. Flinch leaped back, avoiding an untimely end to his career.

"He didn't even see me," Flinch muttered. The driver never glanced at him.

"What a jerk." Looking both ways, Flinch finished crossing the street, then walked back into the hotel.

PART FOUR

which is probably
the most hectic friday
the guys will ever experience

three-part harmony

WHEN I WOKE on Friday morning, Martin was already up, watching TV with the sound turned low.

"I have a perfect plan," he said. "We stay here. The food is great. They have all the good cable channels." He pointed to the TV section from the paper. "There are some cool shows on tonight. The beds are comfortable, and there's a maid to clean up after us. What do you think?"

"Perfect. And when Bowdler catches me and locks me up again, you get to have the TV all to yourself. How about we save that as a backup plan?"

"Okay. If you're going to be selfish, we'll tackle your problem first. But it's fun to imagine living here, isn't it? I mean, you can even get video games right on the TV. How cool is that?" Martin walked over to the window. "Nice view, too."

"It would help if we knew more about them. Hey—you know what? I have their document files." I patted my pocket.

Martin wasn't listening to me. He pushed the curtains aside and leaned closer to the window, pressing his forehead against the glass. "Whoa . . ."

"What?"

"Someone almost got hit by a car."

"So?" I figured that happened about once every five minutes around here. The cab drivers and the valet-parking guys seemed to be having a contest to see who could terrify the most pedestrians.

"So he jumped away *before* the car swerved in his direction."

"Like Flinch?" I asked.

"More than like him. I think it *was* him. For a second, I thought I was watching a dodgeball game at Edgeview." Martin jerked his body from side to side, in imitation of Flinch's awesome dodgeball moves. "He went inside. Come on. Let's catch him before he leaves the lobby."

I handed Martin the room key. "You go. I'll wait here." I figured if he saw me in the lobby, he might start shouting. The last thing I wanted was attention.

"Good idea."

Martin headed out. I paced the floor and tried to imagine his progress through the hotel. If Flinch was here, that would be great. Martin was smart, and Flinch was smart, but together they were amazing.

The door opened, and Flinch walked in. He looked like he'd put on some muscle since I'd seen him. He'd gotten a bit taller, too, but still wore the same dreadlocks.

"Hey, dead guy," Flinch said. "How ya doing?"

"Better than ever," I said.

"Flinch was on TV last night," Martin said.

"Awesome."

Flinch walked over, stared at me for a moment, then said,

"What the heck, nobody's watching." He grabbed me and gave me a hug. "Man, I was sick over you dying. It hit me hard." He let go and stepped back.

"I can imagine. It came as a shock to me, too."

A strange expression flittered across on his face. "Are you okay?"

"Yeah."

"You sure? No injuries. No fatal diseases. Nothing deserving immediate sympathy?" The corner of his lip twitched.

"Nope. Why?"

"Because if you were hurting, I'd feel guilty about laughing my butt off." The twitch grew into a grin as he pointed at my hair. "Black is not your color." His whole body shook, and he dropped to his knees. "You look like you asked for a shoe shine when you were standing on your head."

I sat on the bed and waited for him to finish howling. My wait would have been shorter if Martin hadn't joined in. Finally, Flinch gasped, shook his head, and wiped a couple tears from the corners of his eyes.

"Done?" I asked.

"Yeah. No, wait . . ." He snickered, snorted, chuckled a bit, then nodded.

"Did Martin fill you in?"

"Nope. He figured it would be better if I heard the details straight from the corpse's mouth. So, what's going on?"

I told him everything, including the news about Cheater and Lucky. And the part where I killed the guy. When I mentioned that, Flinch shook his head and said, "Wasn't your fault. You were defending yourself."

"Everything I do is my fault," I said.

"If I let myself feel guilty for everything I did," Martin said, "I'd be a mess. Actually, maybe that's why I'm a mess."

"We're all a mess," Flinch said.

"Not you. You're like a celebrity, now," I said.

"Hardly. I'm just one of a billion guys trying to find an audience. Even on the networks, half the comics you see are awful. Besides, who's more messed up than people in show biz?"

"Still, it's totally awesome that you were on TV," Martin said.

Flinch's grin returned. "Yeah. It doesn't seem real. But it's hard to feel happy when my friends are in trouble. Having a hidden talent can stink."

"Being fifteen can stink," Martin said. "Too young to drive. Too young to make good money. Everyone treats you like a kid, but all I hear is 'act like a man.' No way I'd want to act like some of the men I've known."

"I'll take you guys over any adult out there," I said. "Even if you are too young to do anything useful." And for the first time since I'd awakened in the room with the gorilla on the ceiling and the rippling walls, I actually believed I had a fighting chance to survive this mess.

quadratic equations

FLINCH DOVE PAST me, landed on the bed with a belly flop, and shot his arm toward the bedside table. "I got it," he said. As he put his hand on the phone, it rang.

"Show off," I said.

He flashed me a smirk and lifted the receiver. Before he could speak, I yanked the phone from him and shot it across the room to my waiting hand, then returned his smirk as I said, "Hello?"

"Hi. It's me. I saw Lucky again."

"How's he doing?"

"He's spacy. I think they've got him on meds. Probably an antipsychotic, given the listless way he was—"

I cut him off. "I get the idea. Did you talk to him?"

"Sort of. There was a nurse with him, so I had to be careful. I didn't tell him you were alive. I was afraid it would mess up his head." Cheater paused after each sentence. I guess his face was still sore. "But he wasn't completely gone. He was smart enough not to talk out loud. He came over to my bed and thought about what happened to him. At least, as much as he was capable of thinking clearly. Everything

163

was blurry. Like when you try to read the newspaper after it gets wet."

"Did you learn anything?" I asked.

"Yeah. He was somewhere with a whole bunch of lost stuff that he couldn't reach, and he totally flipped out."

"That's rough." I thought about the stress our talents put on us. Next to Lucky, Cheater and Martin probably had it the hardest because they received stuff whether they wanted to or not. I guess it was rough for Flinch, too. I was surprised they didn't all get overloaded.

"I think he takes a couple walks a day," Cheater said, breaking into my thoughts. "I'll keep an eye out for him."

"Great. Do you know how much longer you'll be there?"

"Maybe a couple days. I want to go home now. I feel fine. But you know how doctors are. They want to keep you in the hospital. That's counter-productive. Do you have any idea how many people get sick from being in a hospital? It's called iatrogenic illness. Which is ironic, since Hippocrates's first rule was to do no harm."

After Cheater finished his brief lecture on the history of medicine, I hung up, then told Martin and Flinch what I'd learned.

"Oh man," Martin said, shaking his head. "That's brutal. Lucky always had a hard time coping. But this really stinks. We have to do something for him."

"After we rescue Trash's butt," Flinch said.

Martin pointed at me. "Yeah, your sorry butt is first in line, Trash. And more urgent than Lucky's problems. At least we know he's somewhere safe."

"So Cheater and Lucky aren't in immediate danger." Flinch held up two fingers in a vee. "And we're okay for the moment." He uncurled the other two fingers and extended his thumb. "Which just leaves—"

"Ohmygod!" Martin cut Flinch off. "He's here!"

"Who?" I asked. "Bowdler?" My gut clenched at the thought.

"Not Bowdler," Martin said. "Torchie."

"What?" That didn't make any sense. Torchie lived far northwest of the city, out in the sticks.

"Torchie's in Philly," Martin said

"Of course," Flinch said. "You're right."

"What are you two talking about?" I felt like I'd just walked into the middle of a movie. Make that a foreign movie.

"The pattern," Martin said. "We're all here. Three of us in the hotel. Two in the hospital. But all in Philadelphia. Just like we all ended up in Edgeview. Torchie has to be here."

That sounded too wild to me. "How can you explain something like that?"

"We don't have to explain it," Martin said. "Just accept that there's a pattern. That's what matters. With five of us already here, the hard thing to believe would be if Torchie wasn't here. But I'd bet anything he is." He pointed to the phone. "Give him a call."

I'd lost the sheet I'd printed at the library, but that wasn't a problem. I dialed information, got Torchie's folks' number— there was only one Grieg in Yertzville—and called his house. "Hello. Mrs. Grieg? Is Philip there?"

"Oh, no. I'm sorry. He's out of town. The dear boy really needed to get away. He hasn't been the same since that friend of his died. Andy Thalmaker? Was that his name?"

"Eddie Thalmayer," I said, automatically.

She chatted for a couple minutes, telling me far more than I wanted to know about assorted members of the Grieg family—several of whom had recently been in the hospital or jail—but I also found out what I needed to know. After she was finished, I hung up and told the others, "Torchie's at an accordion convention."

"In Philly?" Flinch asked after he and Martin had stopped laughing.

"Yeah. At some Hillville Luxury Motel."

Martin grabbed the phone book, flipped through it, then read out the address.

"That's not too far from here," I said.

"I'll go get him," Martin said.

"Take a cab. That's kind of a seedy area." I pulled some cash from my pocket and held out a couple twenties.

Martin headed out to get Torchie.

"Why'd you tell Torchie's mom your name?" Flinch asked.

"I didn't mean to." I explained what had happened.

"Just be careful. You don't know who's listening to what." He shook his head. "Man, I'm starting to sound crazy."

"Nope, that's not crazy at all. We have no idea what they might be able to do." I imagined my words moving across the phone lines like a little cluster of yellow sparks. "They probably have all sorts of top secret stuff that most people have no clue about."

"But there's one thing they don't have," Flinch said.

"What's that?"

"Us."

"Let's keep it that way."

About forty minutes later, I heard "Oh Susannah" drifting down the hall, rising in volume from the faint yowl of an unhappy feline to the blaring wail of seventeen injured coyotes. The door opened and Torchie, half hidden behind a huge accordion, staggered in. The half I could see above the accordion looked just the same as I remembered—sweaty red hair, freckles, and the smile of someone who had just been handed a whole bag of Oreos and a gallon of ice-cold milk.

"Hi, guys." He looked over at me. "Man I'm glad you're not dead. How come they said you were?"

"Long story." I gave him the basic details. When I was done, I asked, "What about you? How are you doing?"

"Real good." He put the accordion down on the bed, then said, "Wow. You've got sheets and a blanket."

"And television," Martin said. He tossed the TV schedule from the newspaper to Torchie. "There's some great stuff on tonight."

"You're controlling your power?" I asked.

"Totally. I've hardly burned up anything all summer, except for a tiny part of one cornfield. And our mailbox. But just twice. Oh, and a billboard. I'm real good, unless I get excited."

That's when I noticed the smoke curling up from the newspaper. Flinch, of course, was way ahead of me. He smacked the paper out of Torchie's hand and stomped on it. At the same time, Torchie leaped up, screamed, "Yeooowwwcch," and blew on his fingers.

"Guess I was excited to see you," he said.

"Here, put some ice on it." Martin looked in the bucket. "Shoot. We're out."

"I'll get it!" Torchie shouted. "I love ice machines. They have one where I'm staying, but it doesn't work. And it sort of smells." He grabbed the ice bucket and headed for the door, then turned back. "You guys aren't gonna ditch me, are you?"

"What?" I asked.

"You know. Slip out while I'm away."

"Drat! You figured out our secret plan," Martin said. "I was going to steal your accordion, go back to your motel, and impersonate you. I've been plotting this my whole life. The hardest part was learning to sweat on demand."

Torchie grinned at Martin. "I forgot what a kidder you are."

"Here. Take this." I handed him the key card. Torchie put it in his pocket and walked out.

A half minute later, there was a knock on the door. "That was fast," Martin said. "I guess he had trouble with the lock." He turned the knob and opened the door.

Maybe if it had been Flinch who'd gone to the door, we would have had a chance. But Flinch was busy channel-surfing and Martin never saw it coming. As soon as the door opened, someone tossed a small cylinder through the opening. Before I could react, the cylinder exploded in a cloud of gas.

I tried to open the window, but everything went gray. I could feel myself falling toward the floor. I seemed to be falling forever.

while trash learns that life is a gas, torchie gets some ice . . .

"THIS IS AWESOME." Torchie couldn't believe he was together with his friends again. Sure, they had some problems. People were trying to kidnap Trash. Lucky and Cheater were in the hospital. But there was a bright side to everything. Trash had escaped. Cheater was healing. And Lucky was in a place where he could get help. That was a Grieg family motto: *It could be worse.* Of course, that came true a lot, too. Things got worse. But even then, the motto applied.

Torchie followed the signs, turned several corners, and finally found the ice machine at the far end of a hall. It took him a while to figure out how it worked, but he managed to fill the bucket. And this machine didn't smell. The hotel seemed a lot nicer than the one where he was staying. There weren't any holes in the carpet, and you could see through the windows. He held a piece of ice against his finger for a minute, until it stopped hurting, then headed back.

As he turned the final corner, he looked down the hall and saw a couple guys coming out of Trash's room. Torchie got lost all the time, especially in buildings he'd never been to before. But when Flinch had brought him to the room, he'd noticed the number on the door. It was 427—which was easy to remember because that was exactly what his Uncle Duley weighed last year after Thanksgiving dinner. So the room was right. But something was wrong. The men coming out were pushing a laundry cart. They didn't look like maids.

Pretending he was going to another room, Torchie walked right past 427. He waited until the two men had gone into the elevator, then he went back and unlocked the door. There was nobody there.

"Oh boy," he muttered. "This is not good."

*cell mates

WHATEVER THEY USED to knock us out, I came awake faster than before. No gorillas. No singing crumbs or smiling shoes. But I had a killer headache, and my eyes didn't want to focus. My left arm ached, too. I lifted my sleeve and saw I had a bandage wrapped around my arm, just above my elbow. I guess I'd gotten hurt when they'd captured us. I didn't remember putting up a fight.

I was on a concrete floor. This wasn't the lab house. It looked like a large basement—except part of the space, maybe ten or twelve feet long, had been walled off with iron bars, forming a cell in one corner. There were no windows in the walls. Even without the bars, it would have been a dark, depressing place.

"My head hurts," Martin said.

I looked over to where he was sprawled. "Sorry. This is my fault. I got you into it." I couldn't believe I was a captive again, so soon after escaping.

Flinch was slumped in the corner. His eyes were closed, his mouth hung open, but he was breathing.

"We'll be okay," Martin said.

"And you know that with your psychic powers, Martin?" I shouted.

"Hey, chill out," he said.

"Sorry. It's not you. I'm just angry at everything right now. You have no idea how bad this is about to get."

I clamped my mouth shut as my eyes focused and I realized there was another cell in the corner opposite ours. Someone was sleeping on a cot. An adult. His back was turned to us. There's an old saying Cheater had taught me: *The enemy of my enemy is my friend.* I was still too dizzy to stand. I crawled to the door of my cell and shouted at the guy, "Hey! Wake up!" He didn't move. I tried a couple more times, then gave up and went back to the corner.

A moment later, Bowdler came down a flight of steps to the right of the cells. He didn't have anything in his hand. Maybe he thought I was still too dizzy to be a threat. I waited until he unlocked the door and stepped in. Then I lashed out with my power. I wanted to crack his skull against the bars.

Nothing happened. No satisfying smack of bone against metal. No flying bits of brain.

I scanned the room, looking for the disrupter. Bowdler gave me a thin smile. "Oh, we're not lugging around clunky prototypes anymore. You'd be surprised how small a device we can make. But I'm not here to discuss technology." He glanced toward Martin. "I have the feeling you also have psychic powers."

I remembered the sarcastic words I'd shouted a moment ago. *And you know that with your psychic powers, Martin?*

Bowdler had probably heard me all the way upstairs. "That was a joke," I told him.

"I think not. I think it was the truth. The name 'Martin' does seem to ring a bell. You cried it out the day you escaped." Bowdler crossed the cell and put his foot on top of Martin's hand where it rested on the floor. "The truth?"

Martin shrugged. "You heard him. It was a joke."

Bowdler rocked forward slightly, putting more weight on Martin's fingers. "I don't like playing 'truth or dare.' I much prefer 'truth or pain.' Pain builds character. Something that your generation sorely lacks."

Martin hated bullies. I expected him to spit out an insult or to grit his teeth and refuse to make a sound. I never expected him to talk.

"If I tell you what I know, will you leave the fourth kid alone?" he asked.

Bowdler slid his foot off Martin's fingers, then leaned over and grabbed him by the front of his shirt. "What fourth kid?"

"Nothing," Martin said. "There's no other kid."

"There's nobody else," I said. What was Martin thinking? If Bowdler got his hands on Torchie, it would be like tossing a puppy to a python. I wanted to jump on Bowdler's back and pound him, but I wasn't even sure I could stand up without help.

Bowdler ignored me and pulled Martin closer to him. "Do you know how easily I can make you talk? Do you know how quickly I can have you crying like a baby, just begging me to let you tell everything? Do you have any idea how much of the human body can be sliced off or peeled away without killing someone?"

"You can't . . ." Martin said. "We're just kids."

"Can't what? Look around? Do you see anyone who can stop me? Your little friend, that telekinetic freak of nature, has been tamed. You don't have any way to hurt me, or you would have tried by now. I'm getting bored. So talk."

Don't do it, I thought. *You can't mention Torchie.*

"His name's Dennis Woo," Martin said. "He's in Philly, at the hospital."

"No!" I leaped to my feet, then fell back to my knees as a wave of dizziness washed over me. How could Martin betray Cheater?

"What's his power?" Bowdler asked. "Is he a telekinetic, too?"

Martin shook his head and whispered something to Bowdler. It was too faint for me to hear. Bowdler let go of Martin and strode toward the cell door.

Martin grabbed the bars on the side of the cage and pulled himself to his feet. Grunting with the effort, he dove at Bowdler. Bowdler glanced over his shoulder, then threw back a kick that caught Martin in the gut and dropped him to the ground.

"Looks like I can see the future, too," Bowdler said.

See the future? I had no idea why he mentioned that. Precognition wasn't Cheater's talent.

It didn't matter. Even if he'd mentioned the wrong talent, Martin had broken our vow. Bowdler went out and locked the cell door behind him.

Martin was curled up, but I didn't feel any sympathy for him. "Why'd you do that?"

After all we'd been through, I couldn't believe he'd rat out Cheater that quickly. I know I'd have kept my mouth shut, no matter what sort of things Bowdler threatened to do to me. No matter how many fingers he crushed. I held my hand up, with my palm facing him. "Doesn't this mean anything to you?"

Martin glanced toward the stairs, then whispered two words. "Trust me."

"What's going on?" Flinch asked. He sat up and rubbed his face, then looked around. "Where are we?"

"In deep trouble," I said.

*while trash begins to lose hope, cheater meets a misinformed man . . .

"HELLO, DENNIS." The man pulled the curtain around the bed and sat in the chair. "Your friend Martin tells me you can see the future."

"No, I can read minds." That's what Cheater would have blurted out if he hadn't been trying to avoid moving his jaw so much. As he bit back the words, his brain went from high gear to overdrive.

Obviously, Martin had spilled their secret. But he'd spilled the wrong information. Why? Because Martin must have wanted to bring the two of them together. But why would Martin mention psychic powers? He would never reveal their secret. Which meant it wasn't a secret. So the man knew something. But not the right thing. And he definitely didn't know anything about mind-reading.

Cheater felt like he was holding a weak hand in a game he had to win. He couldn't fold. He had to play it out. Barely moving his lips, he whispered, "I can only see blurry stuff."

"What?" the man asked.

Cheater whispered again, even more quietly, making sure he slurred his words.

The man leaned over so his ear was directly above Cheater's mouth. Cheater opened his mind to the man's thoughts.

This time, it was even harder to keep from blurting anything out. The man had taken Martin, Flinch, and Trash to a building somewhere and locked them up. He was on a mission to find anyone with useful psi talents.

"Where's Martin?" Cheater asked.

"Just tell me about your power," the man said. But the address ran through his mind.

"Sometimes, I can see how TV shows will end," Cheater said.

"What?"

"TV shows. I know what's going to happen before it happens. Five minutes before the ending, it will just come to me in a flash. Even sooner if it's a rerun."

The man straightened up. "That's it?"

"Yeah—that's my special talent. It's spooky. I just know what the future will bring. I guess I'm psychic." Cheater's face was killing him, but he knew he needed to keep talking until the man lost interest in him. "Yup, TV is pretty awesome when you think about everything that's involved. You know, a guy named Philo Farnsworth got the original idea. It came to him when he looked at a cornfield. Amazing, huh? He stares at rows of corn and changes our lives forever."

"Anything else?" the man asked. "Can you see things in the real world?"

"Nope. Just TV shows. But my friends think I'm a genius when we watch mysteries. I've got a TV. Wanna watch something with me? That way, you can see me in action. It'll be fun."

The man shook his head and left the room.

"Bluffed you," Cheater said after the footsteps had faded down the hall. He felt like he'd just won a huge pot with a busted flush. Now all he had to do was figure out how to rescue his friends.

*what's gotten into you?

I'D MOVED AWAY from Martin to the other side of the cell. But Flinch stayed with him. Martin groaned and rubbed his stomach.

"What happened to you?" Flinch asked.

"I got kicked."

"I'd have seen it coming."

"Then maybe you can try to jump him next time while I take a nap." Martin flicked a jab at Flinch's face.

Flinch blinked, but didn't make any move to block the punch. "Do that again."

Martin threw another jab.

"I didn't see it coming," Flinch said.

"Of course not," I said. "There's a disrupter hidden in here somewhere."

"Maybe the field doesn't cover the whole area." Flinch got up and walked to the far corner of the cell, diagonally opposite from where I sat.

Martin got up and joined him. "Yeah, let's check it out."

"Slap me," Flinch said.

Martin took a shot at him, but Flinch blocked it easily enough. "I definitely saw *that* coming."

Flinch took a tiny step toward me, then nodded at Martin, who tried to slap him again. They repeated the process a couple times, until they were several feet from where they'd started. Then, the slap landed.

"Ow!" Flinch said.

"Sorry. You didn't see it coming?" Martin asked.

"Obviously not," Flinch said, rubbing his cheek.

"So the disrupter is on my side of the cell," I said. "If you can get out of the field, I can, too. It looks like Bowdler isn't as smart as he thought."

I stood up and joined them in the corner. Since I hated to miss out on all the fun, I took a swing at Flinch, and smacked him in the cheek.

I was too surprised to say anything. Flinch always sees it coming. My hand never should have landed.

"Oh man, this is bad," Martin said. He looked over at Flinch.

"Yeah," Flinch said. "Really bad."

"What?" I asked.

They both looked at me like they'd just found out I had cancer. An instant later, my body shuddered as I realized what their expressions meant.

"The disrupter is moving with me."

It was on me. Or . . . in me? I lifted my sleeve and stared at the bandage on my arm.

"That truly stinks," Martin said. "I'm gonna stomp that

guy, first chance I get. Starting with his fingers, and ending with his head."

I unwound the bandage. There was a gash on my arm sewed together with crude surgical stitches. Beneath the stitches, my skin bulged as if something had been forced under it. I grabbed my arm to rip open the wound and pull out the disrupter. But just touching the flesh sent such a jolt of pain through me that I let out a scream.

"You guys have to do it," I said.

Flinch shook his head. "No way. You could bleed to death."

"We have to get rid of it." I felt my pockets. All I had was my MP3 player and my wallet. Nothing sharp enough to cut the stitches.

"It won't be easy," someone said. "But you have to try to get it out. Or Bowdler will own you forever."

The voice came from across the hall. I looked toward the other cell, and saw a face I saw every time I closed my eyes. It was a face that lived in my nightmares. "Oh my god . . ." It couldn't be.

*while trash is gasping, bowdler is digging . . .

BOWDLER WENT FROM the hospital to his apartment. He'd have preferred to use the computer at the lab, but the lab had been compromised. Its location could have been revealed by Eddie during the time he was loose. Unlikely, but Bowdler hadn't survived so long by taking chances. That was rule number one: always have a backup. A backup plan, a backup weapon, a backup location. Fortunately, he'd had the foresight to establish several other locations, including the one where the captives were currently being held. Bowdler couldn't help smiling when he thought about the former—and perhaps future—use of the building.

His apartment was outside the city. Nobody knew its location. It took time to get there. But there was no rush. The captives weren't going anywhere. Before he got to work, he took a moment to admire his newest purchase—a hat that had belonged to General Patton. The bidding had been fierce, but he'd won. There was no way he would have allowed such a prize to fall into the hands of some undisciplined hobbyist who had no idea what it meant to be a general.

Nobody beats me. With great care, he put on the hat. Then

he sat at his computer and logged into a program that wasn't supposed to exist.

He entered two names: Edward Thalmayer and Dennis Woo.

Three minutes later, the information he wanted scrolled onto the screen:

```
Commonality #1
Search requests during a single session were made
for:
Anderson
Woo
Grieg
Dobbs
Calabrizi
Thalmayer
Click for details.


Commonality #2
Edward Thalmayer and Dennis Woo
Listed on a prior roster at Edgeview Alternative
School.
Click for details.
```

The hunt was on. Bowdler entered the first two names in the computer, along with the four new last names. All six came up with one commonality—Edgeview Alternative School.

Bowdler made a phone call. "Cover the alarm systems for

me. I've routed everything over to you. I may be tied up for a few hours."

"Do you want me to go there?"

"No need. They're secure."

"What about our little problem?"

"Maybe it's time he disappeared."

"Just say the word."

"No. This one I'm saving for myself. But I'll let you watch."

*while bowdler digs, cheater gets another visitor . . .

CHEATER IMAGINED HIMSELF coming to Trash's rescue in widescreen Cinemascope action, choreographed by wire-work stunt wizard Yuen Wo-Ping. He flew through the air, kicking down the door like a karate master and disarming a gang of bad guys in a blur of feet and fists.

"That would be so sweet . . ."

But this wasn't a time for fantasies. He looked over at the phone for the hundredth time. *Call the police? Call the FBI? Call the newspaper?* Cheater knew he had to make a decision. But none of the choices seemed right.

At least I'm feeling better, he thought. His face still hurt, and his ribs ached, but the pain was easing. It was all bearable as long as he remembered not to talk too much.

Even so, he couldn't help gasping when Torchie came running into his room. "Where'd you come from? Why are you carrying an accordion? I've never seen one that big."

Torchie spilled out an avalanche of words about a hotel, ice cubes, and bad guys with a laundry cart. After he'd finished, and paused to gulp down some air, he added, "How are we gonna find them?"

"I know where they are," Cheater said. "We have to get them out of there. The guy who locked them up is freakin' crazy. I've never been inside a mind that was that dark and twisted. But we'll do it." Together, he knew they could rescue the guys. Synergy was a powerful force. Together, the guys from Edgeview were more than the sum of their parts.

"When are they letting you out?" Torchie asked.

"Right now," Cheater said. "Though they don't know that, yet." Wincing, he sat up at the edge of the bed.

*captive audience

THE LAST TIME I'd seen him, blood was gushing from his mouth. "I thought I'd killed you."

"I'm a tough old coot," he said. "Plenty of nastier people have taken a shot or stab at me, and I survived. But you came closer than any of the professionals." He nodded his head toward me, as if to acknowledge my deadly skills. "I'm Don Thurston."

"You're not dead . . ." It still hadn't completely sunk in. From the moment the memory came back to me, I'd thought of myself as a murderer. The guilt had colored everything I did. It was with me when I woke, and when I went to sleep. I'd taken a life. The weight of that burden had slowed my reactions when I'd had a chance to stop Bowdler.

"No, I'm not dead. Not yet."

"Why are you locked up? I though you were one of them."

"I was. But I never would have handled things the way Bowdler did. He and I are opposites in far too many ways. The whole scenario was wrong—faking your death, keeping you prisoner. I was out of action while that was happening. After I got patched up and saw the way they were treating you, I told Bowdler how I felt. That was a mistake. From then on, he made sure I didn't have direct access to you. I had to think of some way to help you escape."

"Help me escape?" What was he talking about? Nobody had done anything for me. Unless . . . "The medication?"

"I replaced it with water. I figured when you got out of that stupor it would be easy for you to escape. I just hadn't counted on Bowdler realizing I played a role in your awakening."

So he'd helped me get free, and I'd blown it. Now we were both locked up. "What's going to happen to us?"

"Me? I'll probably just disappear once he decides I'm not of any value. I'd have vanished already if he was sure he could get away with it. I still have some friends out there who'd be upset if they thought I'd been canceled."

"What about me?"

"Bowdler plans to turn you into the perfect weapon."

"No way. I'm not doing anything for him."

"You'll do everything for him," Thurston said. "His whole background is in psychological warfare and brainwashing. Believe me, if he wanted to, he could convince you to jump off the Statue of Liberty, or shoot your best friend."

I refused to believe I'd ever do what Bowdler wanted. "He's had me locked up for months, and I still won't obey him." My parents had certainly sent me to enough psychologists without changing anything.

"That was before he had the disrupter. You can't break a will that isn't there. Bowdler needed to keep you safely drugged until he had a way to neutralize your power. Now that you have a clear head and no way to hurt him, he can start working on your mind. You're a tough kid, but he'll break you into a thousand pieces, and then build you back into whatever he wants."

"What about my parents? Are they okay?" I asked.

"As far as I know. They left the country. It's rough that they think you're dead. That's another part of the plan I didn't agree with. I didn't see you as a dangerous weapon that could turn on us. I saw you as raw talent that would probably be eager to help your country. Most boys your age are patriots."

He was right. I was a patriot. But that raised another question. "How could the government treat us this way? I might be a kid, but I have rights."

Thurston stared at me for a moment across the dark corridor that separated our cells. "What makes you think Bowdler is with the government?"

*while trash is learning the truth, torchie and cheater rush to the rescue . . .

"IT'S LOCKED," TORCHIE said. He twisted the door knob again just to make sure.

"Of course it's locked," Cheater said. "Open the lock."

"How?"

"I don't know. Burn it."

"I can't burn metal," Torchie said.

"How do you know? Have you ever tried?"

"No."

"So try."

"Okay, but stop shouting at me."

Torchie glanced over his shoulder to make sure nobody was coming down the street toward them. He didn't think that would be a problem. The buildings on the street looked empty. "Are you sure this is the right place?"

"Absolutely." Cheater pointed to the faded lettering on the canopy that still covered the walkway. "KRAUS FUNERAL HOME. I read it right out of Bowdler's mind. Now hurry up."

"Don't rush me." Torchie scrunched up his face, stared at the lock, and tried to make it catch fire.

"Nothing's happening," Cheater said.

"I know. Give me a minute. It's not like it's a piece of paper." Torchie took a deep breath, stepped back, and tried harder. The doorknob started to glow.

"You're doing it!" Cheater shouted.

The glow faded.

"Please stop talking," Torchie said. He was pretty sure he had the technique now. He gave the knob a full-power blast.

Wummmppfffff.

With a sound like a gas grill lighting, the whole door burst into bright-orange flame. A wave of heat washed over Torchie's face, drawing a flood of sweat from his forehead. The fire only lasted for an instant. Then it faded, leaving the door looking darker than before.

"Wow. That was fast. Talk about spontaneous combustion." Cheater reached forward and touched the surface of the door with the tip of one finger.

The whole door collapsed in a pile of ashes. The knob, with the key-plate and bolt still attached, fell with a clatter, bouncing down the steps like the world's most badly designed Slinky.

"That'll work," Cheater said. "Come on. Let's rescue them." He jumped through the opening, throwing an awkward flying kick, then let out a shout of pain as he landed.

Torchie sniffed the air. Beside the smell of burned wood, he noticed something else. A sharper smell. *Plastic,* he thought. Torchie was familiar with the way just about anything flammable smelled when it burned. He looked up and saw the melted remains of thin red and black wires at the top of the door frame. *Probably for the doorbell.*

Feeling pleased that he'd opened the door without attracting attention, Torchie followed Cheater into the building.

*give me five

"**I FIGURED BOWDLER** had to be from the government. He has all these resources. Everyone who was after me looked like some kind of government agent."

Thurston shook his head. "Manpower isn't that expensive. There are plenty of thugs with guns looking for work. You can hire someone to do anything—even guard a captive kid without asking questions." He waved his hand around us. "This place is nothing, considering the size of Psibertronix's budget."

"Psibertronix? Who are they?"

"You heard of the cold war?" he asked.

"Sure. When the US and Russia were trying to destroy each other without dropping bombs." I'd had that in social studies. The space race was part of the cold war—with both countries trying to get some sort of military advantage. And there was all sorts of spy stuff. Tiny cameras. Deadly poison hidden in the tip of an umbrella. Secret codes. Double and triple agents. Stuff that would have seemed super cool to me before I'd gotten that dart in my neck.

"We were way ahead of Russia in electronics," Thurston

said. "Russia was far ahead of us on psychic research. For the most part, our military and intelligence agencies ignored paranormal phenomena. Almost nobody believed in it. But a group of researchers persuaded the Pentagon to fund experiments in the hopes that we could use psi powers to win the cold war."

"I thought you said it wasn't a government group."

"Not now. Back then it was. Bowdler and I headed a unit that was part of a joint project run by the CIA and the Army. I was brought in because I'd helped uncover some of the Russian secret projects. Bowdler was brought in because of his background in psychology and mind control. We were especially interested in remote spying. But we investigated all sorts of other wild stuff—we tried to walk through walls, knock out animals with our minds, develop immunity to toxic gas."

"What did you discover?" I asked.

"Nothing. We never made any real progress. When the cold war ended, the government cut our funding. Bowdler was the one who suggested we could form a private company. He realized he was at a dead end in his Army career. He wanted to be a general some day. They wanted him to go away. But the military was happy to fund our research, even if there was only a small chance we'd ever find anything."

"But when I got caught, they had the bank photos. That had to be connected with the FBI."

Thurston nodded. "Just because we aren't part of the government doesn't mean they don't cooperate with us. All the agencies share information with us. When the FBI got involved with the bank case, they didn't even notice you on the video. But the officer who investigated the case marked it as 'unexplained' so the file came to us. We took a lot closer look at all the surveillance material than anyone else had. They weren't looking for psi. We were. Well, I was. Bowdler didn't really believe."

"He didn't believe?" Flinch asked, stepping up to the bars next to me.

Thurston shook his head. "He was a total skeptic."

Behind me, Martin said, "Someone's upstairs."

"How do you know?" Flinch asked. "You suddenly develop new powers?"

"Nope. I heard a thump. But from the way they're stumbling around, I think my idea turned out to be brilliant. And I sense an apology coming my way in the near future." Martin flashed a smug look in my direction.

I glanced up at the ceiling, then back at Thurston. I wanted to learn as much as possible before we were interrupted. When Dad was going into a business deal, he dug up everything he could find out about the guy on the other side—even his hobbies and favorite charities. "If Bowdler didn't believe in psi, why did he start a company?"

"The same reason lots of people start companies. Money. We got a nice research budget from the military. That was fine with me. I believed in what we were doing. Not Bowdler. He was just getting back at them for not promoting him. He was totally unprepared when we discovered you. I suspect that's why he didn't turn you right over to the government. He needed to figure out a way to pull the most profit from our discovery. It looks like he's decided to offer a package deal. You're the weapon, he's the controller."

"There's definitely someone upstairs," Martin said. "It sounds like they're searching the place. Which means they're not the bad guys." He turned toward the stairs and shouted, "Hey! We're down here!"

A moment later, I saw Cheater and Torchie lurch into view. Cheater was a bit wobbly, but he looked okay. Torchie was wobbly, too, since he was carrying his accordion.

"How'd you get in?" I asked.

"I torched the door," Torchie said, grinning. "That was hard work. I gotta sit down." He moved past the cell door and slumped to the floor by the side wall.

"You're supposed to thank us for rescuing you," Cheater said. "I figured out what Martin wanted me to do as soon as that creepy guy showed up."

Behind me, Martin cleared his throat. "Anyone want to apologize for doubting me?"

I had something more urgent to deal with. "The front door?" I asked, thinking about the alarm at the lab.

"Yeah, we came right in the front," Cheater said. "What's the big deal?"

"You'd better find the key to this cage real fast," I said. "I think you set off an alarm."

Before Cheater could do anything, I heard more footsteps on the stairs. Heavy, adult steps. A big guy came down, gun in hand. With his other hand, he removed a pair of sunglasses from his face and put them in his shirt pocket. His expression was chillingly blank, like he didn't care what he found at the bottom of the stairs.

synergy

BEHIND ME, I heard Martin gasp, then whisper, "He's a hired killer. That's the guy who was at your house. I called the cops on him, but I guess it didn't do any good."

Keeping the gun on Cheater, the guy held out a large key. "Unlock it," he said.

Cheater took the key and turned toward the cell. I looked around the room. Martin, Flinch, Cheater, Torchie, and me. We had powers that could stop this right now. But our powers were useless while this disrupter was buried in my arm. Torchie was our best bet. But he was right next to me, in range of the disrupter. He'd have to move back past the guy with the gun before he could do anything. We were powerless.

No, that wasn't right. Only our psychic powers had been disrupted. We were bonded together by a lot more than that. Martin must have had the same thought. "We're still a team," he said as Cheater put the key in the lock.

"We just have to cut that thing out of your arm," Flinch said, his voice louder than normal.

They both looked at me. I knew what we had to do. So did they. Now we just had to get the message to Cheater.

"If they hadn't sewn this thing in my arm, you'd be in big trouble right now," I said to the guy.

He laughed and said, "If I hadn't eaten breakfast, I'd be hungry. 'Ifs' are worthless, kid. Get tough and swallow a big mouthful of reality."

I looked over at Cheater, hoping he'd gotten the message. *Come on, we're a team.* Even if the disrupter wasn't working, he was too far away to read my mind. But he was close enough to me in other ways to understand what I was trying to tell him. Time seemed to crawl as I waited for Cheater to act.

He turned the key, pulled open the door, then tossed the key to Martin. As Martin caught the key, Cheater spun back toward the man, held his hands up in a karate stance, and shouted, "Hi-ya!"

I yanked off my shirt and closed my eyes. I felt someone grab me from behind. An instant later, there was a searing pain in my arm so agonizing that I started to pass out. I wanted to flee the pain, but if I lost consciousness, we'd be doomed for sure.

I forced my eyes open. Martin was sawing through the stitches with the key. His own face looked so pale, I could see the veins beneath his skin. I guess Flinch was holding me, because I felt strong arms wrapped around me, pinning my arms to my side.

In front of us, the big guy was staring at Cheater like he was some sort of annoying insect. He pointed the gun at him. "Out of the way. Now."

Cheater waved his arms around and shouted even louder. "Hiiii-Yaaahhhh!"

"Hurry." I tried to say it calmly, but it came out as a scream.

The guy stepped forward, grabbed Cheater by the shirt with his left hand, and tossed him aside like he was made of straw. Cheater let out a howl of pain as he hit the floor. Now the gun was aimed right at me.

I spotted motion out of the corner of my eyes. Torchie rose to his feet, squeezed the accordion shut, then rushed forward and rammed the guy with it. The guy grunted and staggered a couple steps. He must have felt like he was hit by a small truck. But he didn't fall or drop the gun. I knew we only had a second.

"Get it out of me!" There was blood spraying from my arm. Martin's hands were shaking.

"I can't," he said.

"Do it! Or Bowdler will control all of us."

Martin reached into my open wound. As I turned my eyes away, I felt a pain that made the rest of it seem like a gentle kiss.

"Got it," he said.

"Crush it." I slumped against the wall as my legs gave out on me, then slid to the floor.

"No. We need it."

Martin dashed through the open cell door and ran toward the steps. I had no idea what he was doing.

The guy pushed Torchie away, spun around, and aimed the gun at Martin. Between them, Cheater started to get back on his feet. Praying that Martin had moved far enough away, I reached out with my mind and twisted the gun in the guy's hand, turning it back toward him. It would serve him right to take one of those darts in the gut.

He must have held on to the trigger as the gun twisted. The shot was loud. Too loud to be a dart. He grunted like he'd been kicked hard in the stomach, doubled over, then crumpled. The gun slipped from his fingers as he hit the floor.

I studied the open gash in my arm. It didn't seem real. I felt I was watching someone else's blood spill from my veins.

"Torchie," Cheater said, "cauterize the wound."

"What?" Torchie asked.

"Heat it. Seal off the blood vessels. Just be careful—you don't want to cook his arm."

Torchie turned toward me. His face grew even paler than Martin's. But he swallowed hard, and I felt a warmth in my arm. The bleeding stopped. I pointed at the guy on the floor, who seemed dazed enough that he wouldn't be a problem any time soon. "Him, too."

"Him you can fry," Flinch said. "He's one of the bad guys."

"Nobody's totally bad," Martin said. "Help him, Torchie."

While Torchie stopped the guy's bleeding, I unlocked Thurston's door. I felt like I'd just played about seventeen straight games of tackle football with people twice my size. As soon as he got out of his cell, Thurston picked up the gun that the guy had dropped and put it in his pocket.

"Hey, can we turn this thing off?" Martin called from down the hall.

"Pull the battery," Cheater said.

"I don't see one," Martin said.

"There won't be a regular battery," Thurston said. "It's probably bio-thermal—powered by body heat. Check upstairs for a remote switch. Look for a small transmitter. Something with one button and an antenna."

Flinch ran upstairs and came back a moment later with a device the size of a pen. He pushed the button, then told Martin, "Okay, let's check it out."

Martin brought the disrupter over to me. I swung the cell door back and forth with my mind. "It's off," I said. "What the heck were you doing?"

"Saving a friend," he said.

"But you could have just stomped on it," I said.

He shook his head slowly, then smiled. "You aren't the only one of us in trouble."

I realized what he was thinking. "That's perfect."

He nodded. "Yeah, it is."

"Is everyone okay?" I asked as Martin wrapped the bandage back around my arm.

Cheater nodded. Torchie got up from the floor and gave his accordion a squeeze. It made a sound like a newborn kitten. "I think it's broken."

"I kind of like it that way," Flinch said.

"It's definitely an improvement," Martin said.

"What do we do about him?" I asked, pointing to the guy who'd gotten shot. "Should we call an ambulance?"

Thurston knelt down, rolled him over, and examined the wound. "Bullet went clear through. He's okay, short term. Just in shock right now. He'll need medical care eventually. Or we can leave him here to die."

"No we can't." I knew what sort of stain that would put on our souls.

Flinch shrugged. "After what those people did to you, it seems fair."

"We still can't," I said. "But I don't want them chasing after me. Or chasing any of you, for that matter."

"He's no problem," Thurston said. "He just works for the highest bidder. Bowdler hasn't told him anything more than he needs to know."

"So who knows?" I asked. That was the crucial question. If too many people knew about me, there was nothing I could do but run, or accept that my talent doomed me to a future doing things I didn't even want to think about. If it was just a couple people who knew, there was hope.

"Bowdler and I are the only ones who've seen you in action," Thurston said. "The lab workers were never allowed to observe anything. But Bowdler made a video the last time he applied for funding."

My heart sunk at the thought that there was proof of my secret. "What's on it?"

"Just enough to show that telekinesis might exist," Thurston said. "A couple marbles rolling."

Move the marble a half inch, Eddie. Just a nudge. Stop! That's far enough. Wait. Now, very slowly, move it back. I remembered a video camera on a tripod.

"The Russians had lots of that," Cheater said. "I saw it in a documentary. There were all these grainy black-and-white films. Some guy would be staring at a piece of paper and it would flutter. It always looked sort of fake—like he was breathing on it, or there were hidden wires."

"Maybe they'll think the video with Trash is fake," Martin said. "Most people don't believe in psi."

The thought of fake videos and grainy images jammed together in my mind. I remembered that day at the bank, when I'd taken the money from the vault, and I saw a way out.

"I have an idea," I said.

*upon reflection,
a solution appears

"**YOU'D MAKE A** good agent," Thurston said after I'd explained what I had in mind. "We can do that. Everything we need is at the lab. We just have to put our friend on ice for a while."

He grabbed the guy under the arms and dragged him to a cell. "Let's see what we have here." He went through the guy's pockets, pulling out a phone, keys, and a wicked-looking folding knife. He backed out of the cell, then picked up the bloody key and locked the door. "He'll keep for a while. You did a good job with the bleeding."

After we followed Thurston upstairs and onto the street, I dropped back and joined Martin. "Sorry I didn't trust you earlier."

"No problem. I usually don't trust me, either." He pointed ahead and whispered, "You trust him?"

"Yeah. Not that we have to." I tapped Cheater on the shoulder. He moved next to Thurston and said, "You wouldn't hurt us, would you?"

"Of course not."

Cheater put his hand behind his back and flashed us an

"OK" sign. I guess he hadn't found anything dangerous in Thurston's mind.

"You want to check him out, too?" I asked Martin.

"No thanks. I'd rather not learn his deepest secrets. That other guy already spooked me enough. Getting close to Bowdler wasn't a lot of fun, either. He thinks he's the smartest guy on the planet."

When we reached the lab, Thurston pulled a key from his pocket and opened the door. Cheater and Torchie went to scrounge up the parts we needed. The rest of us headed downstairs.

Thurston waited by the door of the room where I'd been kept. I thought I could walk right back in. But I froze for a moment at the doorway, as if I'd hit a force field.

"Take your time," he said.

My hands hurt. I realized I was clenching my fists. I uncurled my fingers, then stepped into the room and stared for a moment at the plain, white walls. Thurston set up the table. The sight of the steel marble made my stomach flutter. I went to the bathroom and washed the blood from my arm.

Martin joined me. "The bad part's over," he said as he scrubbed his hands. "No more blood."

Cheater set the camera on a tripod. Then he and Flinch made sure the angle was just right.

I looked around for Torchie, but he'd wandered off. Martin and Flinch moved aside so they wouldn't be in the shot, and Cheater crawled under the table.

"Ready?" Thurston asked.

I nodded.

He started the camera, then stepped back. I stared down at the marble and put my hands to my temples like I was deep in thought. The steel marble rolled in a figure eight across the surface of the table. I glanced up at Thurston, who mouthed the word, "Again."

We did it a couple more times. Then Thurston stopped the recording. We took the camera upstairs and played the video through a monitor. It looked like I was moving a marble on a table with the power of my mind. But the open door of the bathroom was also in the frame, along with the mirror above the sink. You could see something in the mirror. At a glance, it seemed innocent enough.

"Zoom in on it," I said.

Close up, in the reflection of the bathroom mirror, you could see Cheater's arm under the table, moving a magnet that pulled the steel marble. I thought about the reflection in the bank drive-through window that got me into all of this trouble. Now, a reflection would get me out of trouble.

"Perfect," Thurston said. He pulled the memory card from the camera and put it in his shirt pocket. "I'll see this gets into the right hands. After that, there's no way Bowdler will ever be able to convince anyone that you have powers."

"Will that be enough to make him leave me alone?"

"I intend to be fairly persuasive when we meet, and show him the error of his ways. Bowdler isn't stupid. Besides, he's been sneaking around for months, setting something up. I suspect he has other projects that will bring in more money than he can spend, even if he is trying to buy every over-priced piece of war memorabilia he can find."

"What about the rest of it?" I said. "I'm supposed to be dead."

Thurston smiled. "When you dedicate your career to spreading lies, you also learn how to spread the truth. I can get your resurrection started on Monday. By next Friday, nobody will remember that you were ever dead."

I couldn't believe the nightmare was over. But there was another nightmare I was eager to end. "I need to take the disrupter where it will do some good."

"Give me one more moment." Thurston went to the room with the electronics equipment and pulled a cell phone from his pocket. It looked like the one he'd found on the guy at the funeral home. He took apart the phone, removed one of the chips, replaced it with another that he got from a drawer in the workbench, then said, "Here, hang onto this. We need to stay in touch until I get everything straightened out. It's not traceable through the GPS system, so it's safe to leave it on. The charge should last long enough. Who's good with numbers?"

"I am," Cheater said.

"Memorize this one." He recited a string of digits, then had Cheater say it back. "You can always reach me at that number—day or night. Don't write it down." He handed Cheater the phone.

"What about the guy you locked up?" I asked.

"I'll take care of him as soon as I get my car," Thurston said.

I wasn't sure I wanted to know what he meant by *take care of him*.

Thurston put away the tools, then glanced at the box that held the prototypes. "I hadn't seen this." He picked up the note, then started to sift through the devices. "Maybe there's something useful here."

"Come on." Torchie pointed toward the door. "We'd better get going."

"Relax," I said. "We're going in a minute."

"I'll meet you outside." He picked up his damaged accordion and dashed ahead.

I left the lab with the rest of the guys. As we headed down the street, I asked Torchie, "What was that all about?"

"Nothing."

"Come on. I know you. What's going on?"

He pulled something from his pocket. "Look what I found. I figured it was okay to take it since it belonged to the bad guy. I was afraid the other guy would want it back." He held up a small gadget that looked like a fancy TV remote control. I figured he'd gotten it from the lab.

"Wow," Martin said. "A box."

"It makes a cool sound," Torchie said. "There was a label on it saying it's an FME device, whatever that is."

"Probably frequency modulation," Cheater said. "Maybe something to jam a radio transmission."

Torchie pressed one of the buttons, and a whirring hum filled the air. "That one says CHARGE." He pointed the control at Flinch and pushed the other button. "That one says DISCHARGE." There was electronic chirp. But Flinch had already jumped out of the way.

"Watch out," he said.

"It doesn't do anything," Torchie said.

"FM is just a type of radio signal," Cheater said. "It can't hurt you."

"Some of the stuff I've heard on FM hurts a whole lot." Flinch held his hand out. "Let me see."

Torchie handed it to him. "Promise you won't shoot me?"

"I promise I won't not shoot you." Flinch pressed the CHARGE button, then pointed the device at Torchie and pressed DISCHARGE.

"Hey!" Torchie said as the gadget let out another chirp.

"Will you guys quit playing around," I said. "Put that away. It's just a piece of junk."

Torchie grabbed the thing from Flinch and shoved it in his pocket. "I found it and I'm keeping it."

"Whatever." I headed toward the hospital with the guys.

*major glitches

"**MAYBE YOU SHOULD** sneak back into your room," I told Cheater when we reached the hospital.

"I will. But I want to be there when you give the disrupter to Lucky."

"Sure. I wouldn't want any of us to miss that." I felt so good about this. Of all of us, Lucky was the one who had the hardest time coping. Finally, thanks to the disrupter, he'd have a shot at a normal life.

We walked up to the desk outside the psyche unit. "We're friends of Dominic Calabrizi," Martin said. "We came to visit him."

"He's not here," the nurse said. This was a different woman from before.

"He went home?" Martin asked.

She nodded. "You just missed him. His father came for him about fifteen minutes ago."

"Thanks." We turned to walk off. This would delay things. But even if I couldn't give Lucky the disrupter right away, I was glad he was heading home. Maybe he was getting better. Halfway to the elevator, I stopped.

"What's wrong?" Martin asked.

"Something doesn't feel right." I went back to the desk. "Excuse me," I said to the woman.

She looked up. I realized there was no way she would answer the question I was about to ask. At least not if I asked it straight out. *What did the man look like?* I'd have to find a way to trick the information out of her. "Was it Dominic's father or his stepfather?" I asked.

"I hardly see what the difference is," the woman said.

"Well, I want to know where I should go to see him. Was he about this tall . . ." I held my hand about six inches above my head. "With really short hair and a dark blue jacket."

She nodded automatically. It had been an accurate description—not of any imaginary stepfather, but of our far-too-real enemy. "Thanks."

I spun and dashed for the elevator.

"Bowdler?" Flinch asked.

"Has to be."

"Oh no," Martin said as we got into the elevator. "Bowdler has Lucky."

"It looks like it," I said.

"How?" Martin asked.

"It wouldn't be hard. He had my name and Cheater's name. Maybe he ran them through a computer and Edgeview popped up."

"It would be easy from there," Cheater said. "He wouldn't have any trouble finding out where Lucky was."

"So what do we do?" Flinch asked.

"Thurston should still be at the funeral home," I said. "He can help."

As soon as we left the hospital, Cheater pulled out the cell phone and punched in the number Thurston had given him. He listened for a minute. "No answer."

"Are you sure you called the right number?"

"Of course." Cheater repeated the number.

It sounded familiar to me. I looked at Flinch. He nodded. "That's the one."

"Try again."

Cheater dialed, held the phone to his ear, then said, "Nope. No answer."

You can always reach me at that number—day or night.

"I don't like this." I flagged down a cab. The driver wasn't thrilled at the idea of five kids and a giant accordion in his cab, but a twenty-dollar bill erased his concerns. We crammed in and rode back to the funeral home.

"Do you think Bowdler brought Lucky here?" Martin asked.

I looked at the opening where the door had been. "I can't tell. We're just going to have to go in and find out."

When I went through the doorway, the hairs on the back of my neck rose up.

"Something's wrong here," Martin said.

"Yeah." I walked to the stairs at the end of the hallway. Halfway down, I froze. "Oh God . . ."

"What?" Flinch pushed by me, then lurched to a halt. I saw his whole body shudder. He spun around, staggered past me, then bent over and threw up.

I choked down my own nausea and forced myself to move a step closer. I didn't want to. The chill on the back of my neck grew colder as the odor of spilled blood flooded my nostrils.

"They're both dead," I said.

There'd been a fight. That much, I could tell for sure. I guess the guy put up a struggle when Thurston went to take him out of the cell. I heard a thump behind me. Torchie had dropped to a seat on the steps. His head went limp. As he started to tip over, Cheater steadied him.

"Let's get out of here," Flinch said.

I shook my head. "I have to see . . . Maybe it's not too late. Maybe Torchie can stop the bleeding. Thurston is really tough. I broke all his ribs and he lived."

Martin grabbed my shoulder. "He's gone."

A knife handle stuck out of Thurston's chest. His eyes were wide open and staring. The other guy, outside the door of the cell, was sprawled face down in a pool of blood that was still slowly spreading. I think he'd been shot in the throat. The guy must have pulled a knife and stabbed Thurston. It looked different than the knife Thurston had taken from him earlier. I guess he'd had it hidden. And I guess Thurston managed to get off a shot before he died.

Then I noticed something else. There was blood on the steps below me.

"Footprints," I said. "I'll bet Bowdler brought Lucky here, then took off when he saw the bodies. We probably just missed them."

"Let's go," Cheater said.

"Wait," Martin said. "We need that video."

I looked at him. He looked back at me. I knew neither of us wanted to reach into a dead man's pocket.

"I'll do it." Flinch went down the steps, skirting around the blood, and slipped two fingers into Thurston's shirt pocket. He pulled out the memory card, shuddered, and came back up the stairs.

"You okay?" I asked.

He nodded, then shuddered again. "Must have just happened. He's still warm."

I stared at Thurston for another moment, then turned and went outside. The fresh air scrubbed my lungs, but the rest of me felt smeared with the stink of death.

some dim place

I STOOD OUTSIDE the building and kicked the ashes from the door off my sneakers. "I'm sorry." My words felt hollow. How could anything make up for dragging the guys into this mess?

"Don't apologize," Martin said. "You didn't know this would happen."

"Hey, we've been in trouble before," Cheater said.

"Not like this." My voice sounded flat to me. So did theirs. I think we were numbed by what we'd seen.

Martin shrugged. "Trouble is trouble. We'll be okay."

"It could be worse," Torchie said.

"We don't even have a place to go."

I realized the hotel was out. That's where Bowdler had found us. I hated to leave my stuff behind, but there was nothing I could do about that. We couldn't go to anyone's house. Somehow, they'd connected Lucky to me. Probably through Edgeview. So they knew about all of us. "What's your hotel like?" I asked Torchie.

He wrinkled his nose. "It's not great. I think the guy who

was there before me had a dog. And the room's really small. But I guess we could go there."

"We've got a better place," Cheater said. "My uncle owns a business in Chinatown. That's only about twelve blocks from here. There are apartments above it. He keeps a couple of them available for family members. I stay there all the time."

"Awesome," Flinch said. "I love Chinese food."

Cheater spun toward Flinch. "Did I say anything about food? What makes you think it's a Chinese restaurant?"

Flinch shrugged. "I just figured . . ."

"What? He's Chinese so he must own a Chinese restaurant? Man, that is so racist. If Lucky's uncle had a business, would you assume it was a pizzeria? What about you? If your uncle had a restaurant, would it be a rib joint?" Cheater spat out the last words, then grabbed his face and groaned.

"Hey, sorry," Flinch said.

I looked around, worried that someone would hear the shouting, but there was nobody in sight. That was good. I didn't want anyone to know where we were going.

Cheater led us over to Chinatown, and then down a crowded, narrow street to a two-story whitewashed brick building. I could see red paper lanterns through the window, and all sorts of strips of paper on the walls with Chinese writing. The familiar aroma of egg rolls in hot oil mingled with other tantalizing scents. As we went inside, Flinch said, "Hey, is this your uncle's place?"

Cheater nodded. "Uncle Ray. He's great. He's not my real uncle. He's my father's best friend. I've known him as long as I can remember."

Flinch pointed to the rows of small tables, covered with platters of steaming food. "But you said it wasn't a restaurant."

"Nope. I said it was racist for you to assume it was a restaurant."

Before they could argue any further, we were interrupted by an old guy in a tan shirt and gray suit who rushed over from the register.

"Dennis," the man said. "Are you hurt? What happened to your face?"

"I'm okay, Uncle Ray," Cheater said. He pointed at us. "These are my friends. I was hoping we could stay here for a day or two."

"Are you trying to get away from your brother?"

Cheater nodded. "You know how he is. With the folks on their trip, he thinks of me as his personal servant. So, can we hang out here?"

"Of course. You're welcome anytime. The spare apartment is empty." He pulled a key ring from his pocket, slipped off one of the keys, and handed it to Cheater.

Cheater led us back outside, and then in again through a narrow door next to the restaurant that opened right to a flight of stairs. There were four apartments on the second floor. Cheater unlocked the first door on the right and we followed him in. The place had three bedrooms, a bathroom, a living room, and a kitchen. There were two couches, a dinner table, and a couple easy chairs in the living room. We all collapsed into the cushions.

If I didn't have to move again for the rest of my life, I'd be happy. I just wanted to sink down so deep nobody could find me. Everyone looked totally exhausted. I waited for someone to talk, but nobody else said a word. Finally, I broke the silence. "I never saw a dead person before."

"Me either," Martin said.

"I saw my grandfather at his funeral," Flinch said. "No blood . . ."

"It's like a candle," Cheater said. He blew a hard puff of air. "Poof. Gone."

There was another silence. I could tell that nobody wanted to talk about it. That was okay. There'd be time later.

After a while, Cheater dashed into the kitchen and came back with a deck of cards. "Anyone want to play?"

"With you?" I shook my head. "We might as well leave the cards face up."

"How about slap jack?" Flinch said.

"Only if you play with your eyes closed." I slid the deck out of Cheater's hands, one card at a time, and piled it back up on the table. Then I formed pairs into supports and started building a house of cards. Somehow, it seemed appropriate.

"This is great," Torchie said. "We're together again. I wish I could play some music." He picked up his accordion and gave it a squeeze. It let out a sigh and a puff of air. I watched the cards topple over. He put down the accordion, then pulled the FME thing out of his pocket and pushed a button. It whirred. "At least I've still got this."

"Could you do that someplace else," Martin asked. "The sound is giving me a headache."

"Sure." Torchie went off to the kitchen. Mingled with the

whirs and chirps of the device, his voice drifted out to the living room. "This is really great."

"Yeah, it's great and all," I said. "But the one guy who can help us is dead, our friend has been kidnapped by a psycho, and we don't have a clue what to do."

"Not yet," Martin said. "But when has being clueless ever stopped us?"

I walked over to the window and looked out at Chinatown. I didn't know if it was good or bad that we put people into categories like this, but right now I was glad I had a place to be, even if I wasn't really a part of that place. Cheater came and stood next to me.

"I love this whole area. I've been coming here since I was little." He pointed across the street to a store on the corner. "I used to get candy over there. And the place next to it had the best comic books."

"Hey, candy and comic books. Sounds like the perfect world," I said.

"Pretty much." He pointed to the building directly across the street, and leaned toward me. "I'll tell you a secret. The guy who owns that place—he's got a ton of fireworks stashed in there. It's illegal, but everyone around here knows about it."

"Fireworks? We'd better keep Torchie away from there," I said, glancing toward the kitchen.

"That's for sure." Cheater told me about five or six of his other favorite places on the block. When he finished the tour, he said, "Being here is just like being at home."

"That's something we need to talk about." I went back to

the couch and called everyone over. "I don't think any of you can go home until this is settled. It's too dangerous. Bowdler probably has all our names and addresses."

"I'm not meeting my cousin until Sunday night," Flinch said. "If we need to stay together longer, I can think up something."

"I'm okay for almost two weeks," Torchie said. "I can miss a couple days of camp. And it's not like I can play my accordion right now."

"I'm okay forever," Martin said. "Or maybe even longer."

"I have time," Cheater said. "My brother isn't going to tell my parents he doesn't know where I am."

"All right," Martin said. "What do we do?"

"We rescue Lucky and destroy Bowdler," Flinch said.

"Great plan," I said. "But we have no idea where they are."

"So what do we have?" Martin asked.

I turned to Martin. "He got in your face back at the cell. What did you pick up?"

"He's real proud of his theories about brainwashing," Martin said. "And he thinks he's smarter than anyone else. But he's bummed that he never got to be a general."

"That explains the stars on his buttons. All grown, and he's still playing dress-up. But it doesn't tell us anything that will help us find him." I turned to Cheater. "What about you?"

He shook his head. "I just picked up the stuff he was thinking about at the time. Did you see anything when you searched the lab?"

"Nope. Not while I was there." I pulled the MP3 player from my pocket. "But I've got their computer files."

"I'll go borrow Uncle Ray's laptop." Cheater hopped up from the couch and dashed out the door.

"He moves good for a kid who's been stomped flat," Martin said.

"He'll heal faster running around than staying in some hospital bed," I said.

As Cheater came back with the laptop, the rest of us nearly snapped our necks. The most gorgeous girl I'd ever seen walked past the open door. She had long, black hair that swayed with every step she took, and a body that justified the existence of blue jeans. I felt a tingle of electricity shoot through my tired nerves. She glanced inside the room and smiled at us. Then she must have caught sight of Cheater, because she said, "Oh, no! Dennis, what happened to you?"

"I fell."

"Repeatedly?" she asked. "Or in with the wrong crowd?"

"The latter."

"Bad move. But you're ok?"

Cheater nodded.

"You look good without your glasses."

"Thanks."

The girl turned and headed down the hall.

"Who's that?" I asked.

"Oh, that's just Livy," Cheater said. "She's staying here while she goes to this summer program at the college. She's a second cousin on my mom's side."

"No way." I walked toward the door so my eyes could follow her down the hall. "You two can't possible share any DNA."

"Humans and bananas have ninety-nine percent of the same genes," Cheater said.

"And you're ninety-nine percent bananas." Flinch crowded next to me at the door.

Martin joined us. I heard him gulp. Then he squeezed past us and jogged after her.

"That is so unfair," Flinch said. "He's going to suck up to her with his talent."

"I don't think so," I said.

Before Flinch could ask me what I meant, there was a thud in the hall as Martin tripped over his own feet—with a little help from my talent. By the time he got up, Cheater's cousin had disappeared behind the door at the end of the hallway.

Martin slunk back. I expected him to be angry, but he just sighed. "You probably saved me from making a fool of my-self. How old is she?"

"Sixteen," Cheater said. "But she's pretty mature."

"No kidding. I think she's out of our league," I said.

"If that's how you feel, I'll take the next turn at bat," Flinch said. "Girls love guys who make them laugh."

"I think girls love music," Torchie said. "Heck, everybody likes music." He pulled the FME device from his pocket again.

"Go in the kitchen," we all shouted.

While Martin, Flinch, and I were talking about Livy, and revealing how little we knew about girls, Cheater sat down at the dinner table and plugged my MP3 player into the USB port. "Let's see what we have."

Martin and Flinch crammed in on either side of him. I

leaned over his shoulder and watched. Cheater opened the first file. The screen filled with a jumble of letters.

"It's garbage," Martin said.

"Try another."

Cheater opened the next file, and got another screen full of junk.

"Are you sure your memory didn't get messed up?" Flinch asked.

"I pulled it from the computer without ejecting it. And I've been running all over the place," I said. "It could have gotten damaged. Try some more."

With each file that Cheater opened, my hopes grew dimmer. "So we've got nothing." As I slumped back down on the couch, the phone rang. Cheater picked it up, listened for a moment, then said, "It's Uncle Ray. You guys want to go downstairs and get some dinner?"

I was starving, but I was also exhausted. I'd been gassed, kidnapped, operated on—twice—and dragged all over Philadelphia. I couldn't stand the thought of sitting at a table making pleasant conversation and pretending my life was normal. I looked around at the guys. They seemed pretty fried, too.

Cheater told his uncle, "Maybe I'll just grab some food and bring it up."

"That sounds perfect," Martin said. "I'm not moving another step tonight."

Cheater hung up the phone. Ten seconds later, there was a tap on the door and Livy poked her head in. "Hey, I'm going down for dinner. You guys coming?"

"Yeah!" Flinch said, leaping to his feet ahead of the rest of us.

"Great idea!" Martin said.

I pushed myself to my feet. Sure, I was tired. But it would be rude to turn down an invitation. I went to the kitchen to get Torchie, who was playing with a radio on the counter. "It doesn't work," he said.

"You didn't burn it, did you?"

"No." He sniffed the air. "I didn't burn anything in here. Not yet."

"Forget about it," I said. "We're going to get some food."

We followed Livy down to the restaurant. Uncle Ray was sitting at a big round table in the back, near the kitchen. There were a half dozen platters of food in front of him, along with heaping bowls of steamed rice.

"Come on, boys," he said, "get it while it's hot."

Livy sat next to him. As Martin grabbed the seat next to her, Cheater made the introductions.

"So, what are you studying?" Martin asked Livy.

"I'm taking math courses right now," she said. "But my special interest is video-game programming."

I could see Martin's jaw drop. Mine felt pretty loose, too. Not only was she smart and beautiful—she loved games. That sort of combination could make any guy momentarily speechless.

Torchie broke the gaping silence by telling Livy, "I play the accordion. But mine broke."

Livy didn't seem impressed.

Flinch told a joke.

Livy smiled politely.

"Math's my favorite subject," Martin said. "In school," he added, as if there could possibly be some other place where math was a subject. "Numbers are awesome."

Livy's cheek twitched. I couldn't tell whether she was holding back a yawn or a smile.

I dug through my life for anything that would make me seem irresistibly attractive to a brilliant, beautiful, video-game-playing older girl. I definitely didn't want to earn a yawn. I doubted she'd be impressed by my ability to draw zombies and skeletons. Other than that, I came up blank. So I grabbed a fork and turned my attention to the food, but watched the premier episode of the Martin and Livy show out of the corner of my eye.

When she poured herself some tea, he poured himself some tea. When she picked up her chopsticks, he picked his up. When she ate a piece of chicken, he started to eat one. But just before it got to his mouth, it somehow slipped from the sticks, hit his chest, and rolled down the front of his shirt, landing in his lap.

Martin glared at me. I grinned back at him and tried to act innocent, then turned toward Livy to say something clever. There had to be a great line that involved math or falling food. While I was trying to think of something, Livy laughed and said, "Oops, they are pretty slippery." She reached down with her chopsticks, plucked the piece of chicken from Martin's lap, and held it up to his mouth. "Here you go."

Martin took a bite, then flashed a smirk at me.

Dropsticks! Shoot. I thought of it way too late. I gave up and went back to eating.

As we finished the meal, Torchie looked around the table and asked, "Do you have any fortune cookies?"

"Those are for tourists," Cheater said. "This food's authentic."

"Well, I'm a tourist," Torchie said. "Besides, I like the way they taste."

"Then you should have a fortune cookie," Livy said. She got up and brought back cookies for all of us.

Torchie broke open his cookie, stared at the fortune for a moment, then said, "I don't get it. NEVER FEEL TROUBLE OR IT WILL FOLLOW YOU. What's that mean? Is it like, don't worry?"

"Let me see." Cheater snatched the fortune from Torchie's hand. "It doesn't say 'feel.' It says, 'flee.'"

"Never flee trouble." Torchie nodded. "Yeah. That makes more sense."

The rest of us checked our fortunes. As Martin tried to snap his cookie open, it shattered into a dozen pieces. He shot me another glare, but Livy just laughed again and helped him brush the crumbs off his shirt.

"You're gonna die," he muttered when we headed back up the stairs.

"Get in line," I said.

while the guys are catching their breath, bowdler gets to know his new friend

MAJOR BOWDLER UNSHEATHED the sword and placed the flat side of the blade against the boy's cheek. "This weapon was carried by General Sumner on San Juan Hill. Do you have any idea how special that makes it?"

The boy wasn't listening. He was still under the influence of whatever drugs he had been given at the hospital. That didn't matter. Bowdler was willing to wait. The drugs would wear off by morning. He sheathed the sword and picked up a flight jacket. "This was worn during the Battle of Midway."

He went over to his hand grenade collection, and fondled one of his favorites. "Carried onto the beach at Normandy. Not that you have any clue where Normandy is or why it's important." He sighed and replaced the grenade.

"So, Thurston is dead." Too bad Thurston had killed Granger. He was just about the best freelance operative available, even if his taste in neckties left something to be desired. He knew the meaning of discipline. There were only a couple men who were as efficient, and as cold-blooded. Fortunately, their services were for hire.

Bowdler prodded Lucky with his toe. "I hope you're worth

it. If nothing else, I'm sure you have a lot to tell me about your friends."

Eddie was out there somewhere. But not for long. Bowdler uploaded images of the other four boys to his contact at the counter-intelligence facility. Then he placed a call to a number very few people had.

"Santee?"

"Yes."

"Are you available?"

"For the usual fee."

"Fine. Assemble a team that can neutralize five untrained individuals."

"Terminate?"

"Negative. The goal is abduction. Terminate only as a last resort to prevent contact with the press or any authorities."

"Understood."

Bowdler told the man the remaining details and gave him direct access to his counter-intelligence contact. Santee would be expensive, but it would be money well spent. With him on the job, Bowdler could turn his attention to issues closer at hand. After a good night's rest, and a terrible morning, the boy would be ready to answer some questions.

BOWDLER WOKE, AS always, at 5:00 AM. For the rest of the morning, he shook the boy awake every ten or fifteen minutes, but let him go back to sleep each time. Finally, at noon, he said, "Rise and shine, Dominic. We have a lot to talk about."

"Let me sleep," the groggy boy mumbled.

"You've slept enough."

"When do I get my medicine?"

"Soon. I just want to talk, first."

"I need my medicine."

"You're special, aren't you."

"No."

"All your life. You're not like other people. You're so much better."

"I'm normal."

"You can do things. Tell me when you first knew you were special?"

Patiently, Bowdler began to dig.

Fifteen minutes later, his cell phone rang. *That was fast,* Bowdler thought. He hadn't expected to hear from Santee quite so quickly, but that was one of the reasons the man charged such a high fee—he was frighteningly efficient at what he did. Bowdler flipped open the phone, then paused when he saw the call wasn't from Santee. It was from a dead man.

Running his hand along the polished handle of a Colt .38 pistol that once belonged to General Eisenhower, Bowdler raised the phone to his mouth and said, "Yes?"

contact

I WENT TO bed and slept so deeply I didn't remember my nightmares. I didn't even get up until it was almost noon. I joined the guys in the living room.

"Got any ideas?" I asked.

"This." Martin pointed to the cell phone that was lying on the table. "I'll bet the last call he got was from Bowdler."

"So you think we should try that number?" I asked.

"It can't hurt," Flinch said.

You don't know Bowdler. Even the thought of talking to him made my muscles tense up, which made my arm ache. But Flinch was right. We couldn't just sit around and wait to get caught again.

I picked up the phone and called the number. Whoever answered just spoke one word. "Yes?" It was enough. I recognized his voice. I felt like I was holding a scorpion in my hand. I had to grip the phone hard to keep from flinging it away.

"Let Dominic go," I said.

I heard a small chuckle, like some freakin' movie villain who'd just duct-taped the hero to a large stack of dynamite or the nose cone of a missile. Then Bowdler said, "Or what?"

"Or you'll be sorry." I realized I sounded pretty powerless.

"We could arrange a trade," he said. "You for him. There's so much more we need to do, Eddie. Think about all the good times we had. We could have a lot of fun."

I remembered something my father always said: *Never negotiate from a position of weakness.* Right now, Bowdler had all the advantages. That needed to change. But it had to change quickly. It wouldn't take him long to discover that Lucky's powers didn't have any sort of military use. I was afraid to think about what would happen to Lucky after that—or what was happening to him right now.

"I'd love to chat," Bowdler said. "But I have dozens of fascinating tests to run on a very interesting subject."

The line went dead.

"Well?" Martin asked as I closed the phone.

"He's not going to let Lucky go," I said.

"So what do we do?" Torchie asked.

"We do what we have to," I said. "We go to war."

PART FIVE

**where things
go boom in the night**

corrupt files

I WENT TO the laptop and looked at some of the files. "They can't all be bad," I said.

Martin hopped out of his chair. "I have a great idea. Let's ask Livy to take a look," he said. "I'll see if she's in." He raced for the door.

"Down, boy," I shouted after him.

"It's not a bad idea," Flinch said. "She's smart."

"That's impressive, coming from a guy as smart as you," I said.

Martin returned a moment later, along with Livy, who sat down at the laptop.

"So," Martin said, "can you tell us—"

Livy held a finger up to her lips and shushed him. Then she clicked the mouse a couple times, ran some sort of diagnostic program, and examined the properties of the MP3 player.

"The checksum's okay," she said.

"What's that?" I asked.

"It's sort of like a running total. Basically, it's just a way to make sure none of the data has changed. It hasn't, so we know the files on your flash RAM aren't corrupted. Of course, you could have figured that out by playing some of the music."

"Of course," I said. *If any of us had thought of it.*

She opened one of the files on the computer, scrolled through a few pages, opened several more files, then said, "Hmmmm. That's what I thought."

"What?" I asked.

"It's not bad data. Do you see how it's semi-cyclical? Bad data wouldn't show that sort of scatter pattern. I'm pretty sure it's encrypted."

"Code?" My heart sunk.

"Yeah. Code." She looked at the screen, smiled, and said, "Cool. I really should be studying right now, but I love a challenge."

"It could be a top-secret unbreakable code," Torchie said.

"He's just kidding," I said before Livy could ask why we'd have anything like that. "Can you crack it?"

"Maybe. But it would help if I had a bit of space."

"On the table?" Martin asked, leaning over her shoulder and pushing aside a couple magazines that were next to the computer.

"No, not on the table," she said.

We all took a giant step backward.

"A bit more?" she asked.

We took two more steps back—except for Martin, who took a half step forward. "I'll bet you can beat most guys at video games," he said.

I cringed. Martin might have talent, but he definitely

didn't have timing. Livy didn't bother to respond, even though I suspected she'd just heard him mention one of her deepest prides. She shook her head and went to work, studying the files.

Every minute or two, she'd say, "Ahhh," or, "that's interesting," or "I see," and open another file.

Finally, she looked over her shoulder. "Let me show you what I've found out."

We all moved closer. Livy pointed to three open files that she'd lined up, one above the other, so they just fit on the screen. "Look at these. Based on the file names, they're all business letters. The odds are, they'd have some text in common, especially at the start. At the very least, the header would be the same. And if the first couple words are the same, the coded versions should be the same. But they're entirely different."

She opened several other files. "Same here, with different expense reports."

"So what's that mean?"

"Each file is encrypted with a different key," Livy said.

"Key?" Torchie asked.

"It's like a password," Cheater said. "The letters are used, in sequence, to encode stuff. And you need the same key to decode it."

"So there's no hope?" I asked. There were billions of possible words and numbers that Bowdler could have used.

Livy smiled at me. "Just the opposite."

She let those words hang in the air for a second. Flinch was the first to figure out what she meant. "There are hundreds of files. Nobody could remember a different key for every single one. And if you wrote them down, that wouldn't be good, because someone could find the list."

Livy nodded. "Right. So the key has to be here somehow. But still unique for each file. First, we need a program to test the keys. That's pretty trivial. Give me a minute." She hunched over the computer again and began typing, then glanced up and said, "Space."

We moved back and waited. It took a bit more than a minute, but I don't think any of us minded. She even typed cutely.

"So, smart guys, what's the key?" she asked when she was done.

Martin started to open his mouth when Cheater blurted out, "How about the file name?

"Good thinking, Dennis," Livy said.

"It just popped into my mind," Cheater said as Martin glared at him.

Livy ran her program and clicked on one of the document files. The program asked, "KEY?" Livy used the name of the file. A second later, the screen filled with garbage.

"Nope," she said. "That's not it. But nice try. Any other ideas?"

Martin moved a couple steps away from Cheater. "How about using the file name backward?" he asked.

"Yeah. I like that." Livy ran the program again, and this time typed the name backward.

The screen filled with words. Beautiful, normal, words. "Awesome!" I said.

"You're amazing," Flinch said.

Livy shrugged. "Everybody's got to be good at something."

I thought about the hundreds of files in the folder. "So we just have to do this for each file?"

"Are you kidding? Why go through all that work when you can write a program?"

"Well, maybe *you* can write a program," I said. I didn't bother finishing my sentence. Livy was already back at the keyboard.

"All done," she said, twenty minutes later. "Everything's in plain text, copied onto the hard drive. So, what are you guys doing with encrypted files?"

I was about to try to say something clever, but I realized there was no way I could outsmart her. So I decided to go with the simple truth. "It's a long story," I said. "I can't really talk about it."

I expected her to ask more questions, but she just said, "Okay," and headed for the door. As she stepped out, she looked back and said, "Thanks, that was fun. But I gotta go study."

The door closed. "I think I'm in love," Martin said.

"Can you wait to start a family until after we rescue Lucky?" I asked.

"I'll try."

I sat at the computer and brought up the directory.

Cheater leaned over my shoulder and reached toward the keyboard. "Let me do it. You should sort them by date, first."

"That's a waste of time," Martin said, reaching around

from the other side. "If we sort them by name, it will give us a better picture of what we're dealing with."

"That's totally wrong," Cheater said, wedging in closer, and pressing against my injured arm.

"Ow!" I got up from the chair and backed off from the computer. "Go ahead. You guys do it." As eager as I was to see if there was anything useful in the files, I figured it was best to get out of the way. And, to be honest, I figured that even with the arguing, they'd probably come up with some answers quicker than I could.

I grabbed a pencil and sketched while they battled over the keyboard and looked at the files. Eventually, they both sighed and walked over to me.

"Anything?" I asked.

"He's running a couple dozen experiments," Cheater said. "But not for the military. They're for some companies. But there's nothing in here to help us find him quickly. There are hundreds of documents. I have no idea which ones to look at first. This could take days."

"We don't have days," I said. "Lucky needs us."

"It might not be in code any more, but it's still gibberish," Martin said. "Contractors, subcontractors, holding companies, subsidiaries, non-disclosure agreements, sealed bids. I don't understand all this business stuff."

"The only business I understand is funny business," Flinch said.

"You know I don't have a clue," Torchie said.

"Even I don't understand business," Cheater said. "I think

it's a secret language adults use. What the heck is *binding arbitration?"*

"That's just when two parties agree to have a dispute settled by a third party instead of going to court." As soon as the words left my lips, I found four guys staring at me.

"How'd you know that?" Cheater asked.

"I think it's in my blood," I said.

*taking care of business

I PUT ASIDE the sketches and walked over to the laptop. I didn't know a thing about the military or the government. And I sure didn't know about checksums and encryption keys. But I knew the business world. I thought about the phrases Martin had mentioned. The sound of familiar terms got my pulse pumping. Dad had been telling me stuff about the business world all my life. I grew up surrounded by proxy statements, balance sheets, and corporate flow charts. We ate dinner with tales of price-earnings ratios, executive stock options, and leveraged buyouts.

Maybe I'd inherited some of his talent. Dad could take apart a company and restructure it the way a good mechanic could rebuild an engine. I didn't always pay attention, but I guess a lot of it had sunk in.

I started to sort through the documents. It took me almost an hour to get a handle on everything. Finally, I closed the lid of the laptop and slumped back in my chair.

"Bowdler's company, Psibertronix, wasn't just getting money from the government," I said. "Like Cheater noticed, Bowdler has a couple dozen experiments running, all being paid for by other companies." I remembered the box in the lab, and the note that mentioned "our next round of contracts."

"What kind of experiments?" Martin asked.

"Mostly attempts to find paranormal stuff. But here's the thing. Every single one of the companies was getting paid by the government to run experiments. They'd all gotten government research grants."

Martin shook his head. "I still don't get it."

"Me, either," Flinch said.

I pointed to the laptop. "Can you print a file out for me?"

"Sure," Cheater said. "Uncle Ray has an office downstairs, next to the kitchen."

"It's called 'test_sites.doc.' I cut-and-pasted it together from the information in the research contracts."

Cheater grabbed the laptop and dashed off.

"How can the government waste all that money?" Martin asked.

"They almost have to," I said. "Suppose you had a ten-million-dollar research budget and you only spent fifty thousand. How much money do you think you'd get next year?"

"Fifty thousand?" Martin guessed.

"Right. That's the rule. Use it or lose it. And there are so many different departments, divisions, and agencies in the government. Each one has a budget they have to spend."

When Cheater returned, I pointed to the first entry on the printout. "Look at this. Ganelon Corp. Trace-metal sensitivity to paranormal emanations."

"I've heard of Ganelon," Cheater said. "They were in the

news last year for making defective ammunition for the military."

"Hang on. There's lots more." I continued to read from the list. "Vidkung, Limited. Clairvoyant monitoring of dissident movement. Tichborne and Fawkes Industries. Investigation of Kirlian photography as a quantitative means of judging character. It goes on and on. Twenty-four experiments, running at nineteen different companies."

"Vidkung was in the news last year, too," Cheater said. "Something about bribery."

Torchie yawned. Flinch was pacing. I could see from the way Martin was looking all around the room that he was starting to lose interest. Most kids didn't care about politics or business. Put the two together and you got a deadly combination. I decided to give them the short version.

"They're all owned by the same company." I spread out the three pages of the printout. "Ganelon, Vidkung, Tichborne and Fawkes. All nineteen of them. They're all part of Roth-Bullani Enterprises."

"I've heard of them, too," Cheater said. "Aren't there a couple former senators connected with them?"

I nodded. "Yeah. They're one of the biggest government contractors around. Bowdler is providing them with a way to make a ton of money. And he's making out nicely himself. He sells them the equipment. And he charges a fee for analyzing the results, along with a monthly consulting fee. As far as I can see, it's all pretty worthless research." I looked over at Martin, who knew more than any of us about psychic

phenomena. He'd been studying it ever since he first suspected we had talents back at Edgeview.

"Yeah, those experiments sound sketchy," he said. "They
were doing that Kirlian stuff more than half a century ago.
There's supposed to be some sort of mystical aura around people when you take a picture with a special camera. Nothing
ever came of it. But I still don't see how this helps us get Lucky
back."

I tapped the sheet. "About half of these experiments are
in Pennsylvania, New Jersey, or Delaware. A couple are right
in Philly. We can get to a lot of them. If there's one thing I
know, it's business people. I sat through plenty of dinners
with company presidents, board chairmen, and majority
shareholders when Dad brought them home. The guys who
own companies—there's only one thing they understand."

"A free meal?" Flinch said.

"Nope." I rubbed my thumb and fingers together. "Money.
If Bowdler's experiments start going wrong, and costing those
companies a lot of money, they're going to stop doing business with him. Right now, he has a nice little scam going. If all
of that starts to disappear, he'll be happy to release Lucky just
to get rid of us and patch things up with Roth-Bullani."

"So you're saying we should start destroying stuff?" Martin asked.

"Especially anything with this on it." I pointed to the last
sheet, where I'd pasted a JPEG of the Psibertronix logo at the
end of the list.

"I'm in," Flinch said. "Not that I have any way to wreck

stuff, but I'll be happy to watch you and Torchie cause some damage."

I glanced out the window. "We just don't want anyone else watching us. We'd better wait until dark."

"Which means we have time for some food," Martin said. "Right?"

"Yeah. We might as well eat. It's going to be a long night."

"I'll see if Livy wants to join us." Martin ran out the door.

"I'm not sure if that's really sweet or really sad," Flinch said.

"Maybe both." We went down to dinner, but I behaved this time. I figured Martin had it tough enough without getting splattered by food. If he really wanted to try to get Livy to like him, I wasn't going to mess things up for him. But even without my help, he managed to knock over his water glass twice.

When we got back to the apartment, I picked up the list of experiments. "He's got something running on a cargo ship in the port. I'll start with that. There's a warehouse just south of the city. How about Flinch and Torchie go there while I go to the piers with Martin. Cheater can stay here in case we need to get in touch."

Cheater and Martin nodded.

Flinch looked at the address on the printout. "No problem. I can find that."

Torchie stared at me. "What do you want me to do at the warehouse?"

I grinned. "Do what you do best."

"You want me to burn it?"

"Just whatever area has the experiment. You need to be quick. We have to make sure the fire is over with before any firefighters get there. I don't want innocent people hurt. That's rule number one."

"But how will I know what area to burn?" Torchie asked.

I looked over at Cheater. "Got any binoculars?"

"Nope. But you can buy them cheap all around here."

"Great." I knew from my own experiments that I could move stuff I saw in the distance. I wondered whether Torchie could use his power the same way. "Guess we'd better get two pair."

"Let me get them," Cheater said. "I know where the best prices are."

I gave him some money and he dashed off again.

When Cheater returned with the binoculars, I took them and handed a pair to Torchie.

He headed toward the window, then raised the binoculars in the direction of the building with the fireworks.

"No!" I grabbed his wrist. "Not in here. Take them with you."

"Yeah," Martin said. "Go out and destroy."

"But I'm trying not to start fires," he said.

Cheater patted him on the back. "Just do it. I'll explain Utilitarianism to you when you get back."

"Well, that gives us one good reason not to come back," Flinch said.

We headed out the door and down the steps. "Be careful," I said to Torchie and Flinch as they walked off toward the corner. "People are looking for us."

"You, too," Flinch said.

"Yeah, us, too," Martin said. "So, we're going to go destroy a ship?"

"For starters."

first blood

AROUND 9:00 PM, we caught a bus toward Columbus Boulevard, which runs along the piers. "You really think this will work?" Martin asked.

"It will definitely get some attention."

"Speaking of attention, I think Livy likes me."

"Really?"

"Yeah. She keeps coming over."

"Maybe that's because you keep knocking on her door."

"But do you think she likes me?"

"Hard to tell. You could always use your talent to make her like you."

"I sort of tried that. She doesn't seem to care about compliments. Besides, it would be nice if she liked me for myself. What do you think?"

"I imagine it's possible she could like you for yourself."

"That's what I was thinking." He nodded and sat back. A moment later, he said, "I hope Lucky's okay."

"Me, too. I think he was in bad shape even before Bowdler grabbed him. It's only going to get worse. Bowdler's medicine cabinet contains all kinds of nasty stuff."

"How can people do things like that?"

I shrugged. "Ever read a history book?"

"Not unless there was a gun at my head," Martin said.

"You know what I mean."

"Yeah, I guess I do. We've been killing each other ever since we figured out how to throw rocks."

We changed buses and made our way to the piers. We couldn't get too close to the ships, but I spotted the one that was on my list. It was a cargo ship. Bowdler was running an experiment that was supposed to try to detect any form of aggressive attack before it happened—I guess like an electronic version of Flinch. There were parts of the world where cargo ships were at the mercy of modern-day pirates. The first phase of the experiment involved using a bunch of different instruments to record measurements. It was total nonsense.

As we studied the ship, Martin laughed.

"What?"

"We're about to attack something designed to detect attacks. Don't you just love that?"

"Almost as much as pancakes."

I spotted a metal box about the size of a small car at the front of the ship. The side of the box had Bowdler's Psibertronix logo painted on it. There were a couple different types of antennas sticking out of the top.

"We have to damage the ship," I told Martin, "and make it look like that instrument did it. Any ideas?"

"Fire would be good," he said.

"It would. Too bad Torchie isn't here."

"You could rub two sticks together really fast."

"I knew I could count on you for great suggestions." I studied the box. Even without using the binoculars, I could see a couple thick power cables running to it. Reaching across the pier with my mind, I pulled one of the cables from the box. I jumped as sparks danced in the air.

"You okay?" Martin asked.

"Yeah. I just sort of expected a shock. Like when I grab something hot with my mind, I always expect to get burned."

Another arc of sparks shot from the cable. I turned my attention back to the ship.

"Awesome," Martin said. "This could work out."

I nodded, but didn't say anything. I was concentrating on pulling out the other cable. When I had them both under control, I touched one to the deck and the other to the railing. I could sense the power pulsing through them, like they were giant tentacles. Lights inside the ship dimmed, then flickered.

Pop-pop-pop!

I ducked in panic when I heard gunfire. "Someone's shooting at us!" I lost control of the cables and they both fell to the deck.

Behind me, Martin laughed. "Light bulbs," he said.

I realized he was right. It was just bulbs bursting. That was a good sign that I was on the right track. I thrust the ends of the cables back to the railing and deck. There were more pops, and then one huge WHUMPF! The cables went dead.

"Generator, I'll bet," Martin said. "Remind me never to play Battleship with you."

Smoke drifted from beneath the deck. Even back where we were, thirty or forty yards away, it burned my nose. I could hear people farther down the pier running toward the ship.

"Well, that's not going to look too good for Bowdler," Martin said.

"Nope. And we're just getting warmed up." I headed back to the street.

PHONE CONVERSATION BETWEEN MAJOR BOWDLER AND A FREELANCE OPERATIVE KNOWN ONLY AS "SANTEE"

SANTEE: The targets are still in Philadelphia.

BOWDLER: You've located them?

SANTEE: Negative. Two were picked up by a red-light camera thirty minutes ago.

BOWDLER: On foot?

SANTEE: Exiting a bus.

BOWDLER: Good work. Tighten the noose.

SANTEE: Consider it done.

*night missions

"NEXT?" MARTIN ASKED.

"Office building," I told him. "Bowdler has a system set up in an employee interview room at Tichborne and Fawkes. It records Kirlian images of people who apply for jobs. They're going to take people who get caught stealing from the company or cheating or anything, and compare their scans to everyone else's, so they can figure out ahead of time who might be dishonest."

Martin shrugged. "I could tell them that. So could Cheater. Your average five-year-old can spot a crook, for that matter. But this scanning stuff is just nonsense."

"Yeah. And the scanner is about to malfunction big time."

We managed to get a cab and took it over to the building, which wasn't near any of the bus routes. It was a little after ten when we got there. The place was closed. I looked through the front doors and spotted a numeric keypad mounted on the wall. A tiny red light flashed on its upper right corner. For once, I was happy to see an alarm.

"Let's go over here." I headed across the street and moved behind a parked van.

"What's the plan?" Martin asked.

"I saw this in a movie," I told him. As we hunched behind the van, I unlocked the door to the building and pulled it open. Then I pulled it closed and locked it. I didn't hear anything, but I figured an alarm was going off somewhere.

Two minutes later, a car from a private security force came screeching up to the curb. The guard checked the door. Then he unlocked it and walked inside. After he fiddled with the alarm, he walked down the hallway. About ten minutes later, he came back out, shaking his head. He locked the door and left.

I waited a couple minutes and set off the alarm again. It took three more tries before the guard didn't bother going down the hall. Five minutes after he left, I did it again. But this time, we went inside before I re-locked the door. We waited in a corridor until we heard the guard come in and turn off the alarm.

We searched for half an hour before we found the scanning gear. It was set up in a room with a two-way mirror— the kind they used for police line-ups—and looked like a large, modified movie camera. There was a Psibertronix logo on the side. According to the documents I'd read, Bowdler had charged Tichborne and Fawkes $340,000 for the equipment alone, along with all sorts of charges for analyzing the data. The company had probably billed the government at least twice that much.

"Fire?" Martin asked.

I shook my head. "Nope. We need variety. Maybe if it exploded."

"Got bombs?"

"Sadly, no."

"Then how are you going to do that?"

Good question. Like most guys, I wasn't unfamiliar with things that went boom. I'd played around with firecrackers, and tried a couple experiments that I was lucky to have survived. But I didn't think I could whip up a batch of gunpowder right now.

"It doesn't actually have to explode," I said. "It just has to look like it. Stand back." I pushed Martin into the hallway. Then I turned toward the scanner and started pulling small pieces off it and flinging them into the walls, ceiling, and floor. By the time I was done with the scanner, it looked like a bomb had gone off inside of it.

I stood there, panting. I could feel my pulse thudding in my veins.

"Man, remind me never to get on your bad side," Martin said. "And I thought I had anger issues."

"I guess I was a bit angry," I said. "But that sure felt good."

"What if nobody comes in here for a while?" Martin asked. "Tomorrow's Sunday. We can't wait until Monday to get Lucky back."

"Some people never take a day off." I could remember lots of times when my dad worked all weekend.

"But what if nobody goes into this room? They just use it when there are interviews. Right?"

"Good point. So let's leave a couple small hints that something is wrong." I lifted one of the larger pieces from the floor and hurled it through the two-way mirror. I shot another piece through the window between the room and the hall-way.

"That should do the trick," Martin said. "As long as you don't mind seven years bad luck."

"I think I've already had twice that much."

We left the building, setting off the alarm one last time, and walked around to the side so the guard wouldn't see us. While we waited for him to leave, I checked the street. It didn't look like a great spot to get a cab. We'd probably have to hike five or six blocks before we could flag one down. It was after eleven, and I was getting tired of walking. I glanced over at the parking lot behind the building. It was empty except for a car and two vans, each with TICHBORNE AND FAWKES painted on the driver's door.

"You know how to drive?" I asked Martin.

"Sure. Sort of . . . My sister took me out a couple times. Why?"

"Let's get some wheels." I unlocked the car, opened the doors, and switched on the ignition.

"Cool." Martin slipped behind the wheel. "You've done this before."

"Yeah. I never took a car, but I figured out how to start them. You sure you know what you're doing?"

"Absolutely. I was born to drive." After almost backing into a wall, Martin got us out of the lot and onto the street. "I like this," he said. "It's almost as good as a video game." He turned the wheel left, then right, weaving in his lane. He started swaying from side to side, moving his body in synch with the car. Two blocks later, he said, "Oh boy. We've got trouble."

I glanced over my shoulder. A cop car had slipped behind us. I couldn't tell if they were checking us out or just cruising. "You think they know I don't have a license?" Martin asked.

"I think they know you can't drive straight. But I wouldn't worry about it." I reached under their hood with my mind, pressed down on their radiator cap, and gave it a twist. Steam shot out as the cap came loose. They pulled over to the curb and we drove on.

"I could get used to this," Martin said.

"Me, too." I glanced ahead. "Stop sign!"

Martin stomped on the brakes and skidded to a stop, throwing me forward against the shoulder belt.

"Chill out. I saw it." He looked both ways, twice, then drove on. "We really could have anything we want, couldn't we?"

"Maybe."

"I guess the problem is I really don't know what I want. I mean, in the future. Right now, I want Livy to like me. And I want to rescue your sorry, trouble-seeking butt. But all of that rest-of-my-life stuff, I don't know."

"Me, either." I knew I wanted my life back. I wanted to save Lucky and destroy Bowdler. But beyond that, I didn't have any quick answers.

"Wait," Martin said, "that's not true. I know what I want. I want to drive. I want to drive everywhere. All the time. This is way too much fun to stop." He turned the corner smoothly enough that I barely had to hold on.

I knew what he meant. Driving was power. You could go

where you wanted, when you wanted. No schedules. No routes. No waiting for a bus or a parent.

"I got it! Let's go to Las Vegas," Martin said. "Imagine you at a dice table." He shook one fist like he was shaking a pair of dice, then tossed the imaginary dice toward the windshield. "Winner!"

"Imagine me with a bullet in my brain. I'm not messing with those casino guys."

"Okay, so it's not a perfect idea. But you have to admit, it's fun to imagine." He took one hand off the wheel and tapped the sheet on my lap. "What's next?"

I checked the list. "There's an experiment on the Petain International corporate jet."

"Where's the jet?"

"Philly airport."

Martin stomped on the brakes again. Behind us, someone hit the horn, then screeched around our car, the horn still blaring. "Are you crazy?" Martin shouted. "An airport? You know what kind of security they have there?"

"That's why we have to do it. There's no way anyone could get near the jet, so they'll know it had to be one of the experiments messing up. They'll blame Bowdler."

"Forget it," Martin said. "We'll end up in some tiny room, getting searched in places I'd never dream of hiding anything. I don't know about you, but I have absolutely no desire to have my body cavities explored by some guy with a bad attitude and hairy arms."

"Pull over. I'll drive."

Martin stepped on the gas. "Nope. I might be crazy, but I'm not suicidal. I'll drive. You tell me how to get there."

We managed to find route 95 and get to the airport. After Martin parked, we went into the international terminal and took the elevator up to the arrival area. I figured there'd be lots of people waiting to meet flights, so we wouldn't look out of place. There was a hallway with windows right by the elevators. I moved from window to window, trying to spot any place where there were private jets. It felt weird using the binoculars. I was afraid someone would see me and think I was a terrorist.

Martin finally spotted the jet. "Petain International, right?"

"Yeah. You see it?"

"Yup."

"Where?"

"Heading for the runway."

"Shoot." I looked where he was pointing. There was a jet taxiing toward one of the runways. That was a problem. I didn't want to hurt anyone. But I hated to waste an opportunity. Besides, I wasn't planning anything huge. No fires or explosions. Not here, around all this jet fuel and all these people.

I focused the binoculars so I could see into the cockpit. There was a small box mounted in front of the copilot. It had the Psibertronix logo. I yanked it free and bounced it off the instrument panel.

An instant later, the plane stopped moving. I could see the pilot talking on the radio. Then the plane turned down a side path and taxied back toward the hangars.

"Someone's not going to be happy," Martin said.

"Yeah. This will get their attention. If you own your own jet, you expect to go wherever you want, whenever you want. These guys don't like to wait for anything."

"Like if you can drive, you lose the ability to wait for a bus."

"Exactly." I glanced out at the runway. "That felt kind of wimpy, didn't it?"

"Yeah. Not much of a bang."

I thought about what we'd done so far. There were probably already ripples spreading toward the people in charge. But I wanted to make sure I sent at least one unmistakable message. "I'd love to end the night with something more impressive." I looked at the list again, then showed it to Martin. "What do you think?"

He smiled and poked his finger at the last entry on the second sheet. "This?"

"Yeah. I think so."

"It's a bit of a drive," Martin said, grinning. "But I guess I can force myself to get behind the wheel again."

last ups

EVEN WITH THE help of the map that was in the glove compartment, New Jersey was a lot harder to find than the airport. By the time we got to Cherry Hill, it was after midnight. The whole way there, Martin kept singing driving songs. At least, he sang when he wasn't swearing.

"I take back what I said about wanting to drive all the time," Martin said. "These people are freakin' crazy. I can't believe we aren't crumpled up in a burning wreck on the side of the road. Hey, didn't you already die once in a stolen car?"

"I'm trying not to think about that."

"That would be weird, wouldn't it? Dying for real the same way they faked your death."

I nodded and tightened my seat belt. Cars flew past us on both sides. Trucks pulled right onto our tail, even when Martin moved over to the slow lane. I think they'd have driven over us if they could manage that without scratching their nice chrome grills. After a while, I stopped looking out the back window. I just didn't want to see what was there.

We finally reached our exit. I figured it wouldn't be hard

to find Ganelon Corp., since the road looked pretty short on the map. Sure enough, the factory was down by itself at the end of the road, behind a tall fence topped with barbed wire. We parked at the curb and walked over to the fence. The gate was padlocked, which wasn't a problem. Padlocks were easier than door locks.

"This is the company Cheater was talking about. They made the defective ammunition," I said.

"And lots of other stuff that doesn't work," Martin said.

"It's all about to work a whole lot less." I didn't want to deal with any more front doors. We walked around to the side. It was an old building, with paint peeling from the wood near the windows and moss on the walls.

"This place remind you of anything?" Martin asked.

"Yeah. Edgeview." The lights were on, but I didn't see anyone inside. There were windows all along the walls, about four feet off the ground. I figured there was no way they'd put alarms on every window. I unlatched one and raised it, then waited. After fifteen minutes, I decided it would be safe to go in.

I slipped through the opening. Martin followed me in. The place was mostly one big open space, two stories high, with a couple offices in the back on the second level. Machinery and worktables filled part of the floor. Stacked boxes and barrels filled the rest. There was a second room with a big boiler. A large Psibertronix device was sitting on the floor in one corner.

"Let's see what we can do with this." I noticed a valve at the top of the boiler with a gauge next to it. I shut off that valve, then a couple others. The gauge started to move. The side of the boiler made a creaking, groaning sound.

"Maybe we should get out fast," Martin said.

"I agree."

We went back outside and waited. Five minutes passed. Then ten.

"Man," Martin said. "This reminds me of a dud firecracker. You want to check it, but you don't really want to stick your face too close."

"I know. But I guess the boiler had some sort of safety mechanism. Come on, let's take a look."

I was still twenty feet away from the building when the windows in the boiler room blew out. It wasn't much of an explosion.

"That's it?" Martin asked.

"I guess."

"Uh oh . . ." he said.

"What?"

"They make ammunition, right?"

The sight of all those boxes and barrels flashed through my mind. *"Run!"*

Before I could even turn around, the whole side wall exploded with a blast so loud I didn't even hear the second half of it.

I barely had time to close my eyes before the debris smacked my face. Martin and I both got knocked flat. As we were falling, I gave him a shove, to try to get him as far away from the building as possible.

There was a series of smaller explosions that I felt more than heard. I stayed down until I was sure it was over.

"You okay?" Martin asked. He brushed bits of glass and wood off his forehead as he walked back over to me.

At least, I think that's what he said. My ears were ringing. I nodded. "You?"

He nodded back, then pointed to the car.

That seemed like a very good idea.

"Wow . . ." I said as Martin started to turn the car around. "That was big."

"Yeah." He stopped to swear as he hit the curb with the left front tire. After backing into the other curb with the right rear tire, he finally got us headed toward the highway. "That was definitely big. Someone is going to pay attention"

"For sure. I think that's enough for one night. We should bring the car back to where we got it." I didn't want to leave evidence that this was anything other than a bunch of experiments going bad. "If you drop me off where I can get a cab, I'll come pick you up in the parking lot."

"Yeah." Martin glanced over his shoulder toward the building we'd just destroyed. "We might be saboteurs, but we aren't thieves."

"Speaking of which, I wonder how Torchie and Flinch are doing?"

*meanwhile . . .

"PUT IT OUT!" Flinch shouted.

"I'm trying." Torchie clenched his teeth and gave the fire all his attention. The first part had been easy enough. From the hill behind the warehouse, they'd been able to spot a room with the equipment Trash had described. Torchie had set the room on fire and kept the flames from spreading. But he hadn't been able to put out the fire. It was all over the room. Worse, he heard fire engines in the distance.

"Concentrate," Flinch said.

"I can't concentrate when you're telling me to concentrate. And I've never done this through binoculars before."

"Just work on one part at a time."

Torchie squinted his eyes and focused on one wall. The fire dimmed and died. He turned his attention to the floor, but the wall burst into flame again, kindled by the heat in the room. Then the eye pieces of the binoculars fogged up.

Three fire engines raced to the building. Firemen leaped out and started pulling equipment off their trucks.

"Try doing the whole room at once," Flinch said.

"That won't work," Torchie said. "There are too many parts."

"You put out a bunch of fires at Edgeview," Flinch said.

"Those were all little ones." Torchie wiped sweat from his forehead. "These are big."

"I got it," Flinch said. "You can put out a single fire, right?"

"Yeah."

"So let them merge into one fire."

"But the firemen are coming."

Flinch took the binoculars from Torchie. "It won't take long. Hang on. We just need it to spread across the whole wall and meet the floor. Just a second or two. Okay. Try now."

Torchie took the binoculars back, grasped the fire in the room, and made it become not-fire. The flames died, and stayed dead. By the time the firemen broke in, there was nothing to fight but some smoldering wood.

"Good job," Flinch said. "I knew you could do it."

"That makes one of us."

They headed back up the hill toward the street that would lead them, after a long walk, to the cabstand.

"I wish I could drive," Flinch said.

*elsewhere . . .

BOWDLER SLAPPED THE swagger stick into his open palm. He wanted to smack Dominic, but he knew that wouldn't be productive. The boy didn't want to talk. They'd made little progress all afternoon. He just kept saying something about an oath. But he didn't even seem to know where he was. Maybe he wouldn't know who he was talking to.

"Dominic," Bowdler whispered, standing behind him. "It's Eddie."

No reaction. He tried another name. "It's me. Philip."

Still nothing.

"It's Martin."

The boy jerked his head. "I didn't tell anyone."

"Good. I knew you'd keep our secret." Bowdler pulled up a chair and sat behind the boy. It would take a while to extract information. But that was part of the fun.

BY THE TIME the boy passed out that evening, Bowdler felt he had learned every detail of the group. He got up and stretched his kinked muscles. What a discovery—telepathy, mind reading, fire-making. And all of that power would be under his control. Maybe he'd return to active duty. They'd promote him now. They'd have to.

He fell asleep and dreamed of moving the world.

Bowdler woke at 5:00 AM. The phone rang an hour later. It was Santee again. "There have been sufficient sightings to narrow their location to an area south of route six-seventy-six and west of Broad Street. Probably north of Chestnut."

"Chinatown is in that range," Bowdler said.

"Affirmative."

"Give me a minute." He checked the data he'd amassed about Dennis Woo and got the names of his parents. "See if there is anyone cross-linked in any way with William Woo or Sarah Woo. Keep me updated on any progress."

The phone didn't ring for two more hours. When it did, Bowdler was greeted with information he'd never expected.

"There's been a problem with that experiment you installed on the cargo ship," the man said.

Bowdler listened to the report. "I'm sure it's a simple malfunction. I'll have it taken care of next week."

He hung up the phone. It rang again within minutes, bringing more bad news.

*response

IT WAS AFTER 2:00 in the morning when we got back. I was so tired, I just made sure Torchie and Flinch were okay, then passed out in bed. I woke around eleven—about the same time as Cheater. Martin and Flinch were up by noon. Torchie finally woke after one. My arm still ached, and the rest of my body didn't feel much better, but at least my mind was clear.

"No calls?" Torchie asked when he got up.

"Not yet. It's going to take a bit of time. Things move slower on Sunday. But the people in charge of the companies have probably already been to the accident sites. They should be able to figure out right away that Psibertronix was involved."

"If they're smart enough," Cheater said.

"They're smart enough," Flinch said. "They might be evil and greedy and heartless, and they might be happy to rip off the government whenever they get a chance, but they didn't become zillionaires by being stupid."

I nodded. "Yeah. As soon as each company makes the connection, they'll be all over Bowdler. And he'll know it was us. But he can't tell them that. What can he say? 'Sorry. The telekinetic I kidnapped has a bit of a revenge thing going on.' That wouldn't go over too well."

"We need to be ready when he calls," Martin said. "We need everything figured out ahead of time so we can get Lucky back and make sure Bowdler never bothers any of us again. So, what do we do when he calls?"

"We ask him to bring Lucky to us," Flinch said.

"Or we could just demand that he lets Lucky go," Cheater said.

I shook my head. "No, I want to see that he's okay. And I want to meet Bowdler face to face, so he understands that this is over. We need to figure out a safe place for that."

"I'm on it." Cheater went to the laptop and pulled up a satellite view of Philly. He zoomed down and started scrolling around. "How's this."

I leaned over his shoulder and looked at the screen. He'd found a baseball field. It looked like it was next to a school. "That would work," I said. It was also close enough for us to walk there. I'd realized that every time we took a cab, we left a record. And it was tough cramming all five of us into one cab.

"I like it," Flinch said. "I don't want us to do this indoors, or anywhere crowded where we can't see everything that's going on."

"Well, that brings up a tiny little problem," Martin said. "If Bowdler has a disrupter, we're just five kids with no way to fight back. What if he pulls a gun, or uses another of those gas bombs? What if he has someone hiding with a rifle?"

"I did find this," Cheater said. He opened a file on the hard drive. A diagram filled the screen. "It's a schematic for the disrupter."

"Does that help us?" I asked. "Is there a way to block it or something?"

Cheater shook his head. "Nope. Not as far as I can tell."

"We'll figure it all out," I said. If we had to, we could rush him. But I didn't want it to get down to that. Some of us would get hurt. I remembered how he'd kicked Martin. "There's no way I'm letting Lucky stay with him."

"Whatever it takes," Flinch said.

"No matter what happens," Martin said, "we keep going until we rescue him."

Cheater and Torchie nodded in agreement. I knew all of them would fight to their last breath.

Another hour passed. I checked the phone to make sure it was still on.

"Why don't you call him," Torchie asked.

"It's better if he calls." That's one of the things I'd learned from my dad. In any negotiation, it's best to let the other guy say what he wants first. That was our only advantage. Bowdler had weapons. He had resources. We had time. But not as much as I'd like. A couple days with Bowdler might break Lucky beyond repair.

"All this waiting is making me hungry," Torchie said. He wandered into the kitchen, rustled around in a cabinet, then shouted, "Hey, there's popcorn!"

A moment later, he yelled, "I can't get the microwave to work."

"I'll go," I said. I joined him in the kitchen. The microwave seemed to be dead. There wasn't even a display on the clock. I checked the plug. It was in. "Looks like no popcorn."

"Watch this." Torchie stared at the bag. In a couple seconds, I heard popping. A few second after that, the bag was almost full. And a few seconds after that, it burst into flame.

I slid it into the sink and turned on the faucet.

"I haven't quite gotten the timing right," Torchie said. He tore open the bag and grabbed a handful of soggy popcorn. "Mmmm. Not bad. Sorta like buttery Jell-o. Want some?"

"Maybe later." I went back to the living room to wait for the phone to ring.

By four o'clock, I was starting to get worried.

"He's not going to call," Cheater said.

"He will," I said. "He has to." I looked around at the guys, hoping they agreed.

"I think he's waiting until tonight," Martin said. "Rats love darkness."

"Yeah," Flinch said. "A guy like Bowdler doesn't like to slither out into the sunlight."

At eight, half an hour before sunset, the cell phone finally rang.

*elsewhere . . .

THE MORNING HAD been a nightmare of angry calls. Three separate experiments had somehow gone badly wrong, causing considerable damage. There'd also been a mishap on a corporate jet. Worse, Bowdler had seen a story on the news about a devastating explosion at one of Ganelon Corp.'s facilities. That disaster hadn't been tied to his equipment yet, but he was sure a call was coming sooner or later.

It couldn't be coincidence. Eddie was behind it. He'd been picked up on cameras at the airport and the toll bridge. Bowdler smiled. This just reinforced his belief that Eddie had the potential to become a priceless resource. Imagine what he could do once he was properly trained.

The damage was bad, but Eddie was worth a thousand times more than all of the Roth-Bullani contracts. And Eddie would be under control soon. His inexperience made that inevitable.

Bowdler placed a call to Santee. "I have four locations I know he's visited beside the airport." He read off the addresses.

"I'll have my men check taxi records. It'll take some time."

"Use as many resources as necessary. Cost is not an issue. Has the Woo connection provided any cross-links?"

"Too many. We're sifting through it."

"Call me when you find them."

THE CALL CAME at seven-fifty that evening.

"I've located the targets in an apartment above the Happy Dragon Family Restaurant," Santee said. "We're currently directly across the street from the building."

"On the sidewalk?"

"Negative. I'm off the street."

"Do you have a van?"

"Affirmative. Do you want me to extract them from the building?"

"No. It would be best if you secured them in a less-populated area."

"Agreed."

"Hold your position. I think I can arrange for them to leave cover."

Bowdler looked at the bed where the boy was dozing. "Company's coming, Dominic," he said. "Let's give your pal Eddie a call."

*negotiation

I WAITED UNTIL after the third ring, trying to calm my nerves. Then I flipped open the phone. "Eddie's Wrecking Service."

The slight pause told me I'd scored a point.

"You've caused a lot of trouble," Bowdler said.

"I can cause a lot more. Right now, you can probably still patch things up with those companies. Or find some new partners. But I'd be happy to wipe out the rest of your experiments. You'd never make another dime."

Instead of a reply from Bowdler, I heard a shout of pain. Then he said, "Do you recognize that voice?"

I bit back the angry words I wanted to use. "Hurting him doesn't get you anything." I could feel sweat pouring down my back. I tried to keep my voice calm. "Let him go and all of this stops. You get to keep running your research scams. I get to go on with my life."

"We need to discuss this face to face. Go to Rittenhouse Square," he said. "Call me when you get there and I'll give you an address of a house where we can meet."

I didn't like the way he gave in so easily. And I wasn't

going to play any of his super-spy games. "Not a chance. We're meeting someplace open."

"The square is a bit too public for our purposes," Bowdler said. "There's a park nearby."

"Too many trees."

"So what would you suggest?"

"Maybe a field."

"Now there's a great idea," he said, speaking to me like I was a child. "Do you think the Phillies would let us use their stadium?"

"No. I meant a school field or something."

"In the city?"

Playing dumb, I guided him along and, amazingly enough, he finally agreed to meet right where I wanted—at the ball field Cheater had found. I think Dad would have been proud if he'd heard me.

I turned to the guys. "We're meeting him at nine at the ball field behind the high school." It was a small victory, but it gave me hope.

Torchie glanced at his watch. Then he shook his hand like he was trying to fling water from his fingertips, and studied his watch again. "Darn. It isn't working."

"Don't worry about it. The cell phone shows the time."

"I got a new battery in it last month," Torchie said. "It's my favorite watch. It's my only watch, but even if I had another, it would be my favorite."

I got up from the couch. "Forget the watch. It's not important."

"Everything's breaking," Flinch said. "Your watch. The

microwave. The kitchen radio. Nothing works. It's like someone has the hidden talent to kill electronic stuff."

"Wait!" Cheater said. "Torchie, what time did your watch stop?"

"How would I know that?" Torchie asked.

Cheater grabbed Torchie's wrist and looked at the watch. "That's it. I'll bet it stopped when we were at the lab. That thing you found. What did you say it was?"

"There was a note," Torchie said. "To Bowdler. From one of those companies. It said something about a sample of their new FME thing." He went over to the table next to the couch and picked up the device.

"Not FME," Cheater said. He was so excited now he was almost hopping. "I knew that didn't sound right. You got it backward. It's an EMF gun. It fried your watch when Flinch pointed it at you. And you've been frying stuff with it for the last two days. This is awesome."

"What are you talking about?" I asked.

"Electromagnet fields. An EMF pulse kills microprocessors," Cheater said. "We can knock the disrupter right out."

"If that thing really works," I said.

Cheater took the device from Torchie, charged it, and pointed it at a digital clock on the corner table. Then he pressed the DISCHARGE button. The EMF gun let out a weak chirp.

"It didn't do anything," I said.

"It's losing power," Cheater said. "Maybe if I got closer." He walked up to the clock and tried again from a foot away.

This time the numbers on the clock all turned to eights, and then went dark.

"Yup, it works," Cheater said.

"So we can knock out the disrupter," Martin said. "This is great."

"If we can get close enough." I didn't think Bowdler would let us get too near him.

"I got it," Flinch said. "One of us has to go there first and walk past him. Someone he hasn't seen."

Cheater pointed at Torchie. "It's gotta be you. He's seen the rest of us."

I didn't like the idea. "Bowdler is going to be cautious. He knows there are five guys. Maybe he found a picture of Torchie. It's too risky."

"But he wouldn't be suspicious if it was a girl," Flinch said.

Martin and I protested at the same time. "No way," he said.

"We can't send Livy," I said.

"Of course not," Flinch said. "But we can send her clothes." He looked at Torchie for a moment. "I think they'd fit you."

"What!" Torchie backed up a step and held his hands out, as if to push away Flinch and his ideas. "Not a chance. I'll face Bowdler. I'll face anyone I have to. But not in a dress."

"It doesn't have to be a dress," Flinch said. "A skirt would work fine."

"We'll need a wig, too," Cheater said. "They sell them on the corner." He dashed off.

Torchie looked at me, as if I'd help him find a way out. All

I could do was shrug. "Hey, sometimes you just have to take one for the team."

Cheater returned with a blond wig and tossed it to Torchie, who stared at it like he'd just been handed a warm pile of intestines. "I'll get a skirt from Livy," Cheater said.

"I'll ask her for it," Martin said. He dashed out the door and down the hall. We all crowded around the door to watch. I think he was halfway there before he realized how ridiculous a request he was about to make. Of course, by then it was too late because, somehow, he stumbled and ended up running into her door. I almost felt bad when I saw how hard he hit it. Maybe I should give him a break.

When Livy opened the door, Martin said, "Can we borrow a skirt?"

There was dead silence for a moment. Then Martin blurted out, "It's not for me. It's for Torchie."

"For Torchie?"

There was this pause. I could almost hear Martin's brain spinning desperately in search of an explanation. "He's part Scottish," he blurted out. "There's this parade tonight. He forgot his kilt."

"Oh, that explains everything." Livy laughed and disappeared inside her apartment. She reappeared at the door a minute later and handed a plaid skirt to Martin. "Have fun."

"Thanks." Martin came back, tossed the skirt to Torchie, then looked over at me. "She definitely likes me."

Grumbling, Torchie took the skirt and wig and went to change. "I hate to say it," Flinch said when he came back out of the bedroom, "but you'd make a cute girl."

"Then don't say it." A wisp of smoke curled up from the hem of the skirt. It was a good thing the material wasn't one of those synthetic things that burn real easily. Torchie slapped the fire out and walked over to the window, turning his back on us.

"Cute and hot," Martin said.

"I wish you guys would stop making fun of me," Torchie said.

"I'm sorry." I put my hand on his shoulder. "Relax. We don't want anything catching fire." I pointed to the roof of the building across the street where a small flame flickered. "Like that."

He nodded, then squinted his eyes. The fire went out. I checked the time on the cell phone. It was getting close to nine. "We'd better get going."

As we left the building and crossed the street, Cheater sniffed the air. "You guys smell smoke?"

I sniffed. There was definitely something burning somewhere. "Probably from before," I said. Then a flicker of light caught my eye from above. "Oh no . . ." It looked like there was a fire in the building in front of us—the one Cheater had told me about.

"Fireworks . . ." Cheater said.

FWOOMP!

The night lit up. A rocket shot through the window and slithered into the sky. A zillion others chased after it. Firecrackers exploded and bottle rockets whistled.

"Put it out," I yelled to Torchie.

A man came screaming through the door of the building,

his clothes blazing. He rushed down the steps. Two more burning men followed right behind him. All three were wearing dark blue suits. They ran right past us, pushing between Cheater and Martin. One of them pulled a cell phone from his pocket, but then flung it away when the fire spread to his sleeve. As they turned and raced toward a van parked at the curb, howling and slapping at themselves, the fire on their clothes went out. Torchie must have doused it.

"We have to help them," Torchie said.

"I don't think so," Cheater said.

"It might be better if we didn't," Martin said. "They're the bad guys."

The van squealed away from the curb, bounced off a couple cars parked across the street, and blew through a red light. Headed for the hospital, I guess. Torchie turned back to the building. The fire in the window dimmed and died.

I heard sirens in the distance. "We'd better go."

"I feel awful," Torchie said as we walked away.

"Don't," I said. "They probably did a lot worse to a lot of people."

"It doesn't matter what they did," Torchie said. "It matters what I did. I'm a bad person."

"Hey," Martin said, "that just proves you're a good person. A bad person wouldn't feel anything."

"You think so?" Torchie asked, wiping a smudge of soot from his nose.

"Absolutely," Martin said.

"Besides," Flinch said, "I think you just saved us from a

very bad experience. Now let's go give Bowdler a bad experience of his own."

THREE TIMES ON the way to the school, Cheater stopped and looked over his shoulder.

"What's wrong?" I asked.

"I think someone's following us."

"Yeah," Flinch whispered to me. "It's Livy. She wants her skirt back."

I looked over my shoulder. There was nothing but shadows. I pointed at the school. "I'm more worried about what's ahead of us."

As we walked around the side of the school, I imagined coming face to face with a dozen guys in dark blue suits.

"I wish you could sense people from a distance," I told Cheater.

"That would be nice," Flinch said. "Bowdler could have fifty guys with him."

"I don't think so," Martin said. "From what I've seen inside that twisted mind of his, I think he's going to be by himself. He can't imagine that he'd have any trouble with us. He has a disrupter. He probably has a gun or something. For all he knows, the bad guys back there caught us. He's too full of himself to bring along help. He's used to people following his orders. And there's no way he's going to let anyone see him negotiating with a bunch of kids."

"Let's hope so." I turned to Torchie. "I guess you're on."

*elsewhere . . .

BOWDLER KNEW THAT for most people, there might seem to be little point going to the schoolyard. Santee would have the five boys secured before they got this far. But Bowdler believed in covering every possible outcome. If, by some unthinkable circumstance, Santee failed, then this is where Bowdler would need to be. This sort of careful planning was why he was destined to succeed.

He definitely wanted Eddie back. And he wanted the Grieg kid. That would be useful. Fire from a distance. It wasn't as universal as telekinesis, but it still had powerful potential. Dobbs didn't seem to have much value. Unless he could be made to see farther into the future. It might be worth an experiment or two. Maybe try some extreme threats. But this one—Bowdler looked at him with disdain—he wasn't worth anything.

The mind reader would be valuable. The Anderson kid might be useful, too. Though he looked like he'd be the toughest to break.

But that was all in the future. Right now, he had to stay

focused on the present. They'd be here any moment. And then they'd be his.

"Sparkie!"

Bowdler spun to his right and reached automatically into his pocket. A girl was running across the field toward them.

"Sparkie! Here, boy!"

She ran right up to him. She was so close, he could almost count the freckles on her face.

"Have you seen my dog?"

"No."

"You sure? His name's 'Sparkie.'"

"If he ran away, he's probably dead by now."

"You're mean." She let out a loud whistle, then turned and ran off.

As she disappeared around the school, Bowdler pulled his hand from his pocket. He wouldn't need any weapons tonight.

*showdown

"**OKAY, I DID** it," Torchie said when he got back to us. "Now give me my pants."

"What pants?" Martin asked.

"You had my pants," Torchie said.

Martin shrugged. He looked at Cheater. Cheater shrugged.

"Knock it off and give him his pants." I liked kidding Torchie as much as anyone else, but it would be beyond cruel to leave him in a skirt.

Flinch handed over the pants. Torchie pulled them on under the skirt, then slipped the skirt off.

"Are you sure you got close enough?" I asked.

"I hope so," Torchie said.

We'd find out soon enough. When we reached the back of the school, I saw two people standing near the bleachers at the opposite side of the ball field. Even from a distance, I could tell it was Bowdler and Lucky. The field lights were off, but the back of the school was lit up enough so we weren't in total darkness.

When we were about ten yards away from Bowdler, I reached out and plucked some grass at his feet to test my powers. It worked. The disrupter was disabled. Bowdler was at my mercy. I could rip his heart out right now, and we could all walk away.

"You got your power?" Martin whispered.

I nodded.

"Take him out."

Bowdler walked toward us with Lucky in front of him. Bowdler's hands gripped Lucky's shoulders, as if he was steering him. He stopped a couple of yards from me.

"You okay?" I asked.

Lucky's eyes seemed foggy, but he nodded.

"It's over," I said. "Let him go."

I plucked a button from Bowdler's jacket, just to let him know he'd lost. I couldn't wait to see the look of fear on his face when he realized he didn't have any way to stop me.

"Very clever," Bowdler said. He didn't seem ready to accept defeat. I guess an ego that large needs time to react—sort of like a super tanker.

I plucked a second button from his jacket, floated it up in the air, then bounced it off his forehead.

He didn't even blink. "You're quite a smart boy, Eddie." He took his right hand off Lucky's shoulder.

I plucked the last button and chucked it toward the school.

Bowdler took his left hand off Lucky's shoulder. "It looks like you've outsmarted me. Sadly for you, looks are deceiving."

He draped his hands back over Lucky's shoulders. I was ready to react if he had a gun. My stomach tightened as I saw what he was holding. In one fist, he had a hand grenade. In the other, he had the pin. He tossed the pin to the side, and then laughed.

"Here's the thing," Bowdler said. "With a normal grenade, you've got five seconds. Plenty of time for you to deal with it. Of course, I'd be a fool to bring a normal grenade. I've got the detonator rigged to explode the instant I let go. You can pull it away as fast as you want, but I don't think you can pull it away fast enough to keep from getting turned into Swiss cheese by the shrapnel. Remember, I am the world's greatest, and only, expert on the limits of your powers. I don't think you're fast enough. Want to find out?"

"You're crazy."

He slipped the hand with the grenade inside the neck of Lucky's shirt. "Oh, look. It just got even tougher. Maybe you had a slight chance before. But you really can't pull it away fast enough now."

"You'd die, too," I said.

He shrugged. "We'd all die. You, me, your parents. Your friends' parents."

"What?" I felt the whole meeting was spinning out of control. We'd already won. How could we be losing now?

"If I don't make a phone call in fifteen minutes, a chain of events will be set in motion, ending with quite a few tragic accidents."

"What do you want?" I asked.

"You. I want to finish what I started. I want to turn you into the perfect weapon. Of course, I'll need you to take your medicine again, just for the ride back. Happily, I brought a bottle of it with me. Unwatered, of course."

I thought about yanking the grenade from his hand. But I wasn't sure I could get it away in time. Especially now that it was under Lucky's shirt. When I pictured it in my mind, I saw it exploding instantly, right in my face—tearing all of us into shreds, like one of those horrible videos they show on the evening news.

"If I come with you, you'll leave the others alone?"

"You have my word," Bowdler said.

"No way!" Martin shouted.

"You can't go with him," Flinch said.

They were right. I couldn't trust him. After he had me under control somewhere, he'd go back for the others. None of us was safe. I had to get the grenade away from him.

If I could sit with the guys and talk, we'd come up with a dozen solutions. I'd seen it at Edgeview. Once we grabbed hold of a problem, we refused to let go until we found an answer. That was our true talent as a group. We refused to let go. But I didn't have the luxury of discussing this with them. I had to get the grenade away from Bowdler, and I had to do it now.

"Give up, Eddie," Bowdler said.

"Don't let go," I whispered to myself. And saw the answer. I didn't have to pull the grenade away from him. I didn't need to get rid of it. I just needed to keep it from exploding.

"It's time to take your medicine, Eddie," Bowdler said. He held up a small bottle in his left hand.

"No. It's time to put an end to this." I squeezed Bowdler's fingers around the grenade. Hard.

He yelped and jerked his hand out from under Lucky's shirt. For an instant, a look of panic crossed his face, but then he got control again.

"You do anything to me, your parents are at risk," he said. "There's only one way this can end. You're just kids. There's no way you can beat me. You never had a chance."

"You're bluffing," I said. "Check him out, Cheater."

Cheater walked past me. I froze Bowdler's other arm, and his legs, so he couldn't do anything.

"I don't even need to read his mind," Cheater said. "He's a lousy bluffer. His right eye twitches every time he lies." He moved closer and leaned toward Bowdler. "Yeah. Total bluff. And such a filthy mind. You wouldn't believe the names he's calling you."

Cheater backed away. Bowdler glared at me. "If you love your country, you'd come with me."

"I love my country. I hate what you've done in its name. Kidnapping. Fraud. Lots of stuff I don't even know about. All for money. You're just as bad as our enemies. Maybe worse."

"We need to find the pin," Flinch said.

"Now who could do that?" Martin walked up to Lucky, took him gently by the arm and led him away from Bowdler. "How you doing?"

Lucky groaned, then said, "Not too good. Kinda fuzzy. He made me drink some stuff before we came here."

"You think you could find something for us?" Martin asked.

Lucky nodded, then staggered past Bowdler. He walked four or five feet to Bowdler's left, then bent over and reached down to the grass. He brought the pin to Martin, who put it back in the grenade.

I yanked the grenade from Bowdler's hand. I didn't want to have to worry about it, so I moved it all the way across the field, raised it high in the air, then pulled the pin again and let go of the handle. The grenade exploded instantly.

"Cool," Torchie said.

"Not cool if it happened near us," Martin said.

"You loved that, Eddie," Bowdler said. "You like destroying things. And you're a natural at it. That's why you need to come with me."

"I don't need to do anything. It's over. You've lost."

Bowdler shook his head. "It's not over. You haven't won anything. Face reality, Eddie. You know you have no other choice."

"Shut up!" I lashed out and snapped his nose. I'm not sure which of us was more surprised. His body jerked, but I held his hands out to either side.

Through gritted teeth, he said, "You're just like me."

"No I'm not!" I broke his left thumb. It made a louder snap than his nose. As he winced, I thought about the scanner I'd pulled apart in that office building.

"Just like me . . ." Blood flowed from both nostrils.

"No way." I broke his right thumb. A body isn't held together any better than a machine. I glanced at the guys. I could tell from their faces that they'd stand by me no matter what I did.

"Like me . . ." Bowdler said.

"No . . ." I stood on the verge between violence and mercy. I wanted to hurt him a lot more. I wanted to pull every joint in his body out of its socket and make him my marionette. *Dance for me, Bowdler.* I wanted to pay him back for all that he'd done to me and my family.

But the desire itself made me feel sick. *Count the cost.* That was one of my father's favorite expressions. In all his years of buying companies, in all the business deals he'd told me about, he'd never cost a single worker his job. Maybe, some day, if the time ever came to share my secret with my parents, I'd tell him about this moment. And before I even reached the end of the story, he'd know what I'd decided. The cost was too high.

"Torchie, stop the bleeding."

Bowdler shuddered again as Torchie cauterized his nose.

"So, what do we do with him?" Flinch asked.

"I don't know." I couldn't kill him. It's one thing to lash out in anger. It's another to become an executioner. I couldn't turn him over to the police. There was no way I could testify against him without revealing my own secrets. I couldn't let him go. If he ever got his hands on me, or the guys, he'd do far worse to us than snap a bit of bone and cartilage.

"We have to make sure he never has a chance to hurt any of us again," I said.

"I've got the video," Flinch reminded me.

"We've got a lot of documents," Martin said.

"That's good, but it's not enough," I said. I'd seen it on the news. People did all sorts of bad stuff and never got punished. I had to find some way to show that Bowdler had been behind my fake death. And we had to deliver him to the right place, in the right way. I needed to cover him with so much dirt that he'd never get clean.

"We have to take him to Washington," I said.

"All right!" Martin said. "Road trip!"

"No way. You're not driving any of us anywhere until you get your license."

"Then how?" Flinch asked.

I looked over my shoulder and shouted, "We could use a hand."

"Who are you talking to?" Cheater asked.

"You'll see." Earlier, when we were walking across the field, I'd caught the tiniest motion out of the corner of my eye. He wasn't being sloppy. I figured he wanted me to know he was there.

A moment later, someone came shuffling out of the shadows.

Torchie yelped when he recognized Thurston. The rest of the guys gasped. I wasn't surprised, but I was glad.

"He's dead," Torchie said. "I saw it myself."

"You think we're the only ones with a hidden talent?" I asked.

It had to be that way. No normal person could have survived what I did to him. When I first saw him alive, back when we were locked in those cells, I'd been so happy to learn he wasn't dead—to learn I wasn't a murderer—that I hadn't let myself think too much about it.

"You are a tough old coot," I said when Thurston got close enough so we could speak without shouting.

"But a careless one," he said. "I should have searched our captive more carefully for weapons. If I'd found the other knife, he wouldn't be dead, now."

"At least you're alive."

He nodded. "A stab wound heals a lot quicker than a chest full of broken ribs. But I wouldn't recommend either one."

"Sorry about that," I said.

"No hard feelings. We all strike back when we're attacked."

I pointed past him. "Were you just going to stand there in the dark and watch?"

"You seemed to be doing fine." He pulled a plastic strip from his pocket, then walked over to Bowdler and fastened his wrists behind his back. "Douglas, we need to rethink our partnership."

He patted Bowdler down, pulled a knife from a sheath on his ankle and a gun from a holster on his hip, then said, "I'm not making that mistake again. Fool me once . . ."

"I think I know what to do." I told him my plan. "What do you think? You're the expert."

"I like it. Our friend with the knives lived near here. I'm sure I can find some evidence of his part in faking your death. Guys like that always dream of writing a novel or a film script. He'll have left a paper trail. On a happier subject, this afternoon my contacts in Belgium put your parents on a plane back here. They'll be landing at Philly in about two hours, overjoyed at the news that you're alive."

Thurston led us to the side of the school, where a large, dark car was parked. He popped the trunk and pushed Bowdler toward it. "You don't get to ride with the cool kids."

Bowdler, for once, was silent.

We got in the car with Thurston. "You don't mind dropping him off?" I asked.

"It would be my pleasure. As for you, back to Chinatown?"

"Yeah. Thanks." I didn't bother to ask him how he knew where we'd gone. "Are we really safe?"

"For now. Until you slip up again."

"Maybe I won't. You've kept your secret, right?"

"Mostly. The time or two when someone found out about it, they never got a chance to spread the news."

I didn't follow up on that. I'd had enough espionage and death for the moment. But I could just imagine the surprised look on some bad guy's face when he discovered how hard Thurston was to kill.

Instead, I asked him something I'd been wondering about ever since he'd told me he'd been part of a government project. "Why did you get involved with the search for psi in the first place?"

"What better way to keep a secret than to be the one hunting for it?" Thurston pulled over by the restaurant.

"I'll get the files for you. It'll just take a minute to burn a disk." Cheater hopped out of the car and raced up to the apartment.

"Your parents are on flight seven from Brussels, coming in at eleven PM," Thurston said. "I assume you can find your way back to the airport."

I started to answer, then just smiled and nodded. I guess he knew how I'd gotten Bowdler's attention. Maybe he'd followed us the whole time. I reached out to shake his hand. His grip was firm. As we shook, he stared right in my eyes. I felt he was looking deep down inside of me, to see whether he could trust me with his secret.

The grip tightened briefly. Then he let go. "Take care of yourself, Edward." He glanced over his shoulder to the back seat. "You fellows, too. Don't worry. Our friend in the trunk isn't going to be in any position to bother you again. Now, if you'll excuse me, I have some documents to forge, an apartment to search, and a long drive ahead of me. After which, I suspect I'll have to take a serious look at planning my retirement."

We waited until Cheater came back. Then we got out of the car, and I watched Thurston drive off. As we walked into the apartment, I asked Lucky, "Did the voices ever go away?"

"Yeah. When I was with that guy at the field," he said. "But they came back after the girl ran up to us. I hope she found her dog. She was kind of cute."

"No she wasn't!" Torchie shouted.

While Flinch slapped out a small fire that had burst into life on the living room table, I pulled the disrupter out of my pocket, switched it on, and put it in Lucky's pocket, along with the remote switch. He blinked. Then his jaw dropped.

He looked around, as if something had been snatched out from under his nose.

"Gone?" I asked.

"Yeah."

"Good. Don't worry. This time, they're not coming back."

*winding down

I HAD A little time before I had to leave for the airport. "I still feel bad," I said. "If I hadn't been fooling around at the bank, nobody would have ever known about us."

"Hey, it worked out fine," Martin said. "If you hadn't been fooling around, Lucky wouldn't have the disrupter."

"Any of us could have messed up," Flinch said. "Don't blame yourself."

Torchie picked up his accordion and squeezed a pathetic gasp of a note from it. "I mess up all the time. My whole family does. But things come out okay. I just wish I could make some music."

We hung out, talked, and promised to do a better job of keeping in touch. I gave Cheater money to help replace the appliances we'd fried. Cheater told Torchie he could stay with him at the apartment instead of living in that lousy hotel room while he was at accordion camp. And he told Lucky he could make him another disrupter if this one ever broke. Flinch promised to get us all front-row seats the next time he performed. The four of them said they'd bring Lucky back to the hospital since he was still feeling a little shaky about facing the world right away. We all swore we'd always be there for each other. There was no need to make another oath. Enough blood had already been spilled.

We were interrupted by a light knock. Then the door opened and Livy poked her head inside. "Hey, Dennis, is your cute friend still here?"

Five minds filled with fantasies. I'm ashamed to admit I actually briefly wondered whether I had to meet my parents' plane, or just catch up with them after they got home. Before she could turn me into the worst son in the world, Livy walked over to Torchie, smiled, and said, "Hi. I felt bad that your accordion was broken. I know how important music is. I went to the pawn shop to look for one, but they didn't have any. So I got you something else." She held up a large box.

Torchie reached inside and pulled out a bagpipe. "Awesome!" he said. "Let's figure out how to play it."

"Cool," Livy said.

Torchie and Livy started talking and examining the bagpipe. Flinch slipped over to the table next to Torchie and removed several magazines that had begun to smolder while I stamped out a couple small sparks that had appeared on the rug. Then Flinch came over to me and whispered, "Maybe I should add music to my act."

"Maybe we all should." I realized I was in no danger of missing the plane. I wasn't the guy Livy wanted to hang out with. But apparently, neither was Torchie. After they'd chatted for a couple minutes, she walked over and tapped Martin on the shoulder.

I glanced over at Torchie. He seemed to be perfectly happy

squeezing a cloth bag under his arm and filling the air with the sound of dying cattle.

"So you like to play video games?" she asked.

"Love them," he said.

"Me, too. I usually don't play with guys, because they can't stand losing to a girl. But you've been so nice." She flashed him that smile that made all of us melt. "I think it's so cute the way you keep bumping into things. Most guys try to act so tough and macho, it makes me want to scream. Hey, wanna play some games tonight?"

"Sure," Martin said. "I just have to say goodbye to my friend."

I realized he was right—it was time to say goodbye. It was tough to leave, but I was pretty sure I'd see each of them soon enough.

"It's been awesome," Cheater said as I headed out the door. "All of us together. You know, six is a magic number. It's equal to the sum of its divisors. Not counting itself, of course."

Torchie played something on the bagpipe that might have been a marching song, or the sound of baby pterodactyls being tortured.

Lucky, who was still pretty out of it, said, "Thank you."

"Any time."

"Stay out of banks," Flinch said. "I'm not doing this again. No way."

Martin walked me out. "You ready to get back to the real world?" he asked as I waved down a cab.

"It's not like I have a lot of other choices."

"The offer to run away is still good," he said. "We could go anywhere we wanted."

"Maybe next summer. What about you?" I asked. "You going home?"

Martin fed my words back to me. "It's not like I have a lot of choices. Besides, next to Bowdler, my dad is an angel. Though I might get in a day or two of game-playing before I head out."

"Good idea. Congratulations."

"Hey, what can I say. I've got style, charm, and a telekinetic friend who keeps bouncing me off the floor."

"I'm always happy to help. Want me to throw you up the stairs?"

"Nah. Let's not overdo it."

A cab pulled to the curb and I got in.

Martin stared at me for a moment. He opened his mouth. Then he closed it. Then he sighed and said, "Words fail me."

"Me, too."

The cabbie was only a little better driver than Martin, but I figured after coming this far, I could survive one more wild ride. I leaned back and looked out the side window. Far off in the sky, I could see a jet coming in for a landing. I almost felt I could reach out and ease it to the ground.

Down the road, I knew I'd have to deal with my powers, and figure out my role in the world—how to use my hidden talents, and also my true talents. But not tonight. Not this week or this month. Thanks to my friends, I had time. Tonight, I just wanted to be someone's son.

The naked man found clinging to a street lamp near the Lincoln Memorial early Monday morning has been identified as Douglas Bowdler, a former Army major currently residing in Havertown, Pennsylvania. According to police reports, when Bowdler was first discovered he appeared to be delusional, and repeatedly screamed, "Get the gorilla away from me." There is no evidence he had been anywhere near the National Zoo that day. There is an unconfirmed report that he had in his possession a briefcase containing classified documents as well as other documents that point to a variety of illegal activities, including the abduction and imprisonment of a minor. He was also in possession of a handgun which has been tied to the recent killing of another resident of Pennsylvania. Both the justice department and the military are apparently launching investigations. The boy has been reunited with his parents.

after . . .

CHEATER SUNK INTO the couch and turned on the TV, cranking the volume to drown out the bagpipe music coming from the bedroom. He'd already called his brother and told him he was staying with Uncle Ray until their parents got back.

"*The Cincinnati Kid,*" he said out loud, recognizing the movie. He reeled off the date it was filmed and the cast members. Anyone who knew anything about movies knew that this was one of the greatest poker films ever made.

Cheater looked at the screen for a moment, sighed, then changed the channel. Somehow, poker just didn't seem to be as much fun as it used to. But he'd find something else to challenge his mind and test his talents. Life was full of possibilities.

FLINCH GOT TO the hotel a half hour ahead of his cousin.

"Whoeee, I had a crazy weekend," Devon said. He plopped down on one of the beds.

"I imagine."

"Totally wild." Devon kicked off his shoes.

"Good for you."

"So, how'd the show go?"

"Pretty good, I think," Flinch said. He didn't bother saying anything more. Devon had already fallen asleep. But he smiled. It really had gone well. He felt he'd been right where he belonged—up on stage. And side-by-side with his friends when they needed him. Life was good. Funny, but good. Picking up his notebook, Flinch wrote some ideas for new jokes.

My cousin Devon is so wild . . .

LUCKY COULDN'T WAIT for the nurse to show up in the morning with his medicine. There'd been some excitement when he'd walked back into the ward last night, but nobody wanted to admit that they'd released him to the wrong person, so they just took him back to his room and acted as if nothing had happened.

"I think I'd like to try going without it," he said when she came in.

The nurse nodded and smiled. "Glad to hear it. The doctor has been hoping you'd feel that way eventually."

Lucky was glad to hear it, too. And glad that this was all he heard. He reached in his pocket and felt the gift the guys had given him. Now, he knew he could face the world. Life was no longer an endless struggle against the voices.

MARTIN WALKED BACK inside his house without saying anything. His mom rushed over and hugged him. "Are you all right?"

He backed up, freeing himself from her grasp. "I'm fine."

Across the room, his dad glanced over. "So, did running away solve all your problems?"

"Nope. It didn't solve any of mine." *But it sure helped Trash and Lucky.* He couldn't keep himself from smiling. His grin grew larger as he thought about Livy and the fact that he had her phone number in his pocket.

"Is something funny?" his dad asked. He started to rise from his chair.

Martin shook his head and lost the smile. "Nope. Nothing is funny." Actually, lots of things were funny—Flinch's jokes, Torchie's passion for the accordion, the downfall of corrupt people—but this was no time for an argument.

"Promise me you won't run off again," his mom said.

Martin thought about life on the street. Sleeping in an alley. Feeling so hungry he almost sifted through a trash can. He thought of a killer who had given him twenty dollars and, a couple days later, had ended up with his life drained out on a basement floor. No, life was hard enough without creating more problems. "I promise."

His mom gave him another hug. He was angry that she hadn't tried to come after him. But he understood that she couldn't. And he understood how much she missed him. This time, when she held onto him, he didn't step away.

"I REALLY MISSED you," Torchie said when he got home from camp. The people there had helped him fix his accordion. He couldn't wait to show his mom all the new things he'd learned. And he was even more excited about how good he was getting on the bagpipe.

"I missed you too," his mom said. "But I have a surprise for you." She pointed into the living room.

Torchie went in and looked. "Wow! A piano. Where'd that come from?"

"All the neighbors chipped in," his mom said. "They were afraid you'd hurt yourself walking all around with that heavy accordion. Or get hit by lightning like Uncle Perry."

"It looks expensive," Torchie said.

"They felt it was worth it."

"I've got the best neighbors in the whole world. This is great. And they don't need to worry about the accordion. I've got something a lot lighter to carry around when I play music for them. They're gonna love the bagpipe. So will you."

But he couldn't resist the lure of a new instrument. The bagpipe could wait. Torchie sat at the piano and started figuring out "Oh Susannah." His mom went back to the kitchen, but he managed to play loudly enough for the song to reach her.

He was so happy, he sang along. Life was great. Strange, and puzzling at times, and filled with unexpected bursts of flame and puffs of smoke, but still pretty great.

CORBIN THALMAYER LOOKED across the dinner table at Eddie. Even a week after their reunion, he still couldn't believe his dead son had miraculously been given back to him.

There were so many things he wanted to say. But unlike his wife, who was open about her joy, he'd never been good at outward displays of affection, and he knew that teenage boys were easily embarrassed. Though Eddie had borne the initial barrage of motherly hugs with good grace.

Instead of offering hugs, Corbin Thalmayer talked about a thousand unimportant things, just for the sake of hearing a response or two. Tonight, he'd been telling Eddie about a company he was thinking of buying. "The forest land they own through their subsidiary had been fully depreciated, so it doesn't even affect the balance sheet. The current owners have no idea of the true worth of their company."

He paused to take a sip of water, then glanced down at the files that were spread out next to him. "I'm sorry, Eddie. I don't mean to bore you with all this business talk."

"I'm not bored, Dad," Eddie said. "It's actually kind of interesting." He slid his chair over next to his father and picked up one of the files. "So, what's your strategy? You'll get in touch, but wait for them to make the first move. Right?"

"Right." Surprised, he put his hand on his son's shoulder. Maybe Eddie had a knack for business. Or maybe he'd follow his passion for art. Either way, it was good to have his boy by his side, and good to discover he had so many unexpected talents.

A WORD FROM THE AUTHOR

I NEVER PLANNED to write a sequel to *Hidden Talents*. Yet, somehow, I ended up writing two of them. Let me explain. For a long time, I resisted writing a sequel. I felt I had told Martin's story, and there was nothing left to say about him. But readers kept asking when I was going to write a sequel. Everyone had a favorite character, and wanted to know what happened to him after Edgeview. Eventually, I decided to give it a try. I wrote a book about Martin's first year in high school. It had some great scenes. There was a lot of humor, along with some wonderful characters. But the book, as a whole, just didn't work.

There were various problems with it. Perhaps the greatest problem was that I was worried it wouldn't be as good as the original. I was afraid I'd disappoint my readers, and far too aware that *Hidden Talents* had earned a place on a lot of recommended-reading lists. I felt as if I had a legion of critics looking over my shoulder. This is not a productive situation.

The clock was ticking. The book was scheduled for 2004. But that window came and went. The folks at Tor were wonderfully patient, but I felt I was letting them down. In

a word from the author

November of 2004, I had a long talk with my new editor, Susan Chang, who'd been a delight to work with on my story collection, *Invasion of the Road Weenies*. Inspired by this, and confident that Susan wouldn't let me dig too deep a hole for myself without tossing me some sort of ladder, I decided that the best solution might be to start from scratch. I set aside Martin's story, though I may take another shot at it some day. But I still didn't know what to write about.

Whenever I was asked which of the psi five was my favorite, I always picked Trash. (If I was feeling particularly evil that day, I'd add, "Because he has the power to stop your heart.") The more I thought about him, the more I knew it was his story I wanted to tell. A long time ago, while listening to music that was way too loud and way too modern, I'd written a single dizzying scene—no more than a page or two—with someone escaping from a research lab. It was just an exercise. But when I stumbled across that scene one day, I knew it was the seed from which Trash's story would grow. *What if Trash woke up in a research lab?* It was too powerful an idea to resist. I tossed the scene, but kept the concept.

So that's the story I decided to tell. During the process of writing it, I had a ton of support from my wife, Joelle, and my daughter, Alison. I also had the luxury of being able to get feedback from my good friend Doug Baldwin.

As it became obvious to me that this book was very different from *Hidden Talents* in many ways, I made one other crucial decision. I needed to completely forget about reading lists, expectations, inevitable comparisons, and all of that baggage, and just write the sort of book I love to read. It was time to recapture the solid joy of crafting a rollicking adventure. Time to return to my roots. So I gave it my best shot. I hope you enjoyed the ride.

ABOUT THE AUTHOR

DAVID LUBAR grew up in Morristown, New Jersey. His books include *Hidden Talents*, an American Library Association Best Book for Young Adults; *Flip*, a *VOYA* Best of the Year; and the short story collections *In the Land of the Lawn Weenies* and *Invasion of the Road Weenies*. You can visit him on the Web at www.davidlubar.com.